Pamela Cosman was raised in Los Angeles with three older brothers, with whom she discovered a love for all things engineering and science. She is the author of The Secret Code Menace, a children's fiction book on coding and its unexpected uses. She also wrote Free to Choose STEM, an advice book for teens.

When she's not thinking about her next book, or playing Codenames with her husband and four sons, she teaches electrical engineering at the University of California, San Diego. Recently she's been using eye-tracking glasses to figure out what people are looking at, and also finding better ways to transmit video underwater.

THE HEXAGON CLUE

Pamela Cosman

Ransom

The Hexagon Clue
by Pamela Cosman
Published by Ransom Publishing Ltd.
Unit 7, Brocklands Farm, West Meon, Hampshire GU32 1JN, UK

www.ransom.co.uk

ISBN   978 180047 298 3
First published in 2021

1

SPRAY PAINT

The problem with becoming famous by foiling a gang of bank robbers on the very first field trip of the school year is that it's hard to see how the rest of the year could be at all interesting. Sara looked listlessly at the bulletin board near the principal's office. Her cousin and best friend, Daniel, insisted on checking the flyers there each day as soon as they arrived at school.

"Pick Fruit for the Hungry" urged a new flyer on the bulletin board, while another one read "New Lunch Clubs Start Tuesday".

Sara's stomach registered a sudden pang with the word *Lunch*. She pictured the brown bag perched on the kitchen counter at home and realized she'd forgotten to put it in her backpack.

Daniel took a crunchy bite out of his apple and gestured at the posters with his elbow. "Money-making opportunities."

Daniel was obsessed with earning money, ever since the launch date was announced for the game *Arctic Chill II: Submarine Traitors*.

"The orange picking is for charity," Sara pointed out. "You don't get paid, you do it to help people. Though you might win prizes, like fudge." Sara hadn't eaten much breakfast either. She felt like she could eat a whole box of fudge right now.

"Maybe," Daniel conceded with a frown, "but there are also the lunch clubs."

"Since when is a lunch club a money-making opportunity?" She rolled her eyes at him. "C'mon, the bell's going to ring."

He chucked the apple core expertly into the garbage bin and plucked a flyer for the fruit-picking event from the stack on the table. Sara took a copy of the lunch club flyer just as Kevin Reynolds walked past. Kevin was new to the sixth-grade class. Sara folded the paper and walked after him, trying not to look like she was in a hurry.

Daniel's eyes narrowed thoughtfully as he followed Sara to the classroom. Surely there must be some way of making money from the charity event or the lunch clubs. Orange picking was not exactly a competitive sport, but the flyer said you could have teams of three people picking together. Perhaps he could do something with that.

As she slid into her seat, Sara admired the new decorations on the side wall in the classroom. The student artwork and motivational posters had gone. In their place hung a dozen large posters of jewel-red beetles, alien-looking stick insects, and orange butterflies with black eye-spots.

Sara liked these insect posters much more than the last posters. They had been photographs of mountain scenery with annoying captions such as "Genius is 1% inspiration and 99% perspiration."

"New science topic – Insects – starts today!" Miss Robinson was bubbly with enthusiasm, as usual. "Please turn to page seventy-two."

Miss Robinson started with a lot of numerical facts about insects: the number of legs (six), the number of body segments (three) and the number of different species (a number too big for Sara to even remember).

Sara listened attentively for ten minutes before sneaking a glance at the lunch club flyer – even reading the word "lunch" made her stomach rumble. Students were invited to choose one of the lunch clubs, which would meet for the next six weeks.

The offerings were Drawing Anime, Mosaics, Science of Cooking, and Hip-Hop Dance.

This is not a great set of choices, Sara thought. She would have liked math and science choices. Mosaics club would probably just involve using lots of little tiles to make art designs, or maybe – even worse – it would be about the *history* of using lots of little tiles to make art designs. *Hmmm, maybe Science of Cooking is real science?* she wondered, but she was skeptical. It would probably just be cooking.

During the last round of lunch clubs Sara ended up in the Newspaper Club because she thought that's what Daniel wanted to take, while he'd signed up for Math Club knowing it was her favorite. She wanted to make sure there was no mistake this time. She would have to talk to Daniel about it after class.

"Oh, before I forget," Miss Robinson was saying, "in two weeks, there will be an optional weekend event to pick oranges for the food bank." She held up the flyer with the picture of citrus trees.

"And just think!" she beamed, "what a wonderful opportunity to look for insects! Permission slips are due by Friday if you want to come."

As Miss Robinson returned to her discussion of ants, Daniel had a sudden inspiration. He scribbled on the back of the fruit-picking flyer: "Bet you twenty dollars my team picks more than yours." He folded it into a small wad of paper. When Miss Robinson turned her back to the class he tossed the paper over to Tom, who sat in the row behind him. A minute later, a return note landed on his desk.

"You're on," it said.

At recess, Sara and Daniel found Jared, Sara's older brother, on the playground. Daniel showed him the flyer about picking fruit for charity.

"I bet Tom twenty dollars that I can pick more than he can. Will you two be on my team?"

"Of course," said Sara.

"Sure," said Jared, wondering whether the twenty dollars would be split equally among them if they won the bet. He decided to bring that up later on.

Jared was a year and a half older than Sara and in the seventh grade, but he usually didn't mind spending time with his sister and cousin. They sat on the edge of a low wall, sharing their snacks.

Suddenly, Sara spotted Miss Robinson heading back inside. "I need to ask about lunch clubs," Sara declared. She jumped up and raced off. Miss Robinson disappeared around the corner. Sara rounded the corner and almost crashed into Kevin, who was talking to Miss Robinson.

"Oh, I, uh," Sara stammered, "Sorry! Uh..."

"No problem," he said. He gave her a friendly smile.

"I was just telling Kevin about the Mosaic Club," Miss Robinson said, rescuing Sara from the awkward moment with a smile. "Doesn't that sound like fun, Sara?"

"Oh, yes," Sara said, "that's what I'm planning to do!" *Why did I say that? she wondered, I was going to do Science of Cooking.*

"Excellent, then you can show Kevin where Room 205 is," Miss Robinson said as the bell rang.

After recess, the class worked on poems. They had been working on their poems for a week already.

Sara was not happy with her poem. Miss Robinson told them they could choose any form they liked. Sara had a very orderly mind, so she wanted to write an orderly poem. She wanted the first line to start with 'A' and the second line with

14

'B' and so on. Not only that, but she wanted every pair of lines to rhyme.

They were allowed to write about anything as long as it wasn't vulgar.

Sara wanted to write about Iceland. Although she'd never been there, she knew a lot about it from her Icelandic pen pals. She had stamps and postcards from Iceland. But so far, she couldn't get the alphabetical lines or the rhymes to work out.

For that matter, she wasn't feeling so confident about the Iceland idea either. She wasn't letting anyone see her poem yet.

Daniel, meanwhile, was writing a very free-form poem, which went along with his free-form brain. He didn't worry about rhymes. If two lines happened to rhyme, that was fine. If they didn't, that was fine too.

He was extremely pleased with his opening lines:

Fire, fire, everywhere, sludge and bees and sharpened daggers, And the glowing crystals in the reddish light.

Watch out! The dragon comes! Danger danger! Blast of flame!

Now he was working on the next part, which was all about wild creatures and stormy weather. It was a metaphor for the classroom, he explained to Sara as they walked to lunch after class.

"I don't get it," she said. "Poems should make sense."

"It's art," Daniel said breezily.

Sara envied his confidence. She would rather do math problems than write poems. With math, you knew when you had the correct answer. With a poem, Sara never felt certain that she had it exactly right.

As they followed the flow of kids outside to the lunch tables, they came across a small crowd of students trying to get a look at the wall closest to the tables.

The whole area was cordoned off with yellow police tape.

"What's going on?" Daniel asked a seventh grader.

"Dude, spray paint on the wall," said the boy. Daniel admired his half-shaved haircut and wondered how it would look on him– and whether his father would let him try it.

Two janitors carrying buckets and brushes pushed through the crowd of kids. They started scrubbing off what had been sprayed on the wall.

Daniel was able to make out the words "Light lies about Mist" in blue paint, and what looked like "fume" in green, with maybe a "th" and a few bits of other jagged blue and green letters. Then a teacher told everyone to move away and go and eat their lunch.

"Who would have done such a thing?" Sara wondered aloud.

"Who is being accused of lying?" Daniel

mused, as they sat at their usual table, "How can someone say that *light* lies?" Sara looked longingly at his turkey sandwich, and her stomach growled.

"Drivers can see that wall from the street," Sara pointed out, while wondering whether her stomach was loud enough for others to hear. "So maybe the message was meant for people driving by and not for the school."

Daniel took a big bite of sandwich and then directed his gaze from Sara's stomach to the empty table in front of her, and then to her face. He handed her the other half of his sandwich.

"What kind of fume?" Sara said with her mouth full. "Could it be dangerous to breathe? Is someone mad about pollution?"

It seemed like the whole school was speculating about the mystery. No real information was forthcoming, so the stories got more and more extreme, involving the school principal, an astronaut, fumes coming from the science lab, and an eerie green mist over the hills. No one had ever heard of the school being vandalized before. Well, naturally there was some writing on the bathroom stalls, but no broken windows, or graffiti. That had never happened before, so far as any of them knew.

After the excitement at lunch, math class passed slowly. It was never Daniel's favorite.

Miss Robinson explained about systems of equations with unknown numbers that were called x and y. Daniel wiggled all his toes and looked out the window. He couldn't stop thinking about the mysterious spray-painted message.

At 2:00 p.m., their teacher handed out worksheets, and Daniel groaned. Only twenty more minutes before the day ended. His brain didn't want to think about x or y any more.

Math class would be better in the morning, thought Daniel, *when you're not so tired.* Miss Robinson walked up and down the rows, quietly answering questions and reminding fidgety kids to focus. She paused at Daniel's desk. He looked up from his page and she walked quickly back to her desk and started typing on her computer.

Daniel was having a hard time concentrating. $2x + 3y = 7$ and $x - y = 1$. Miss Robinson glanced up at Daniel, so he quickly looked back down at his worksheet.

Two minutes later, when he checked the clock above her desk, he breathed a sigh of relief. 2:19 p.m. – only one minute left until freedom.

The door opened and Mr. Stevens, the school principal, strode in with a serious expression on his face. Every pair of eyes in the room watched him curiously as he exchanged a glance with Miss Robinson, who nodded.

Principal Stevens walked straight to Daniel's desk and looked down at Daniel's backpack, which lay unzipped on the floor.

Daniel looked down too.

There, in his backpack, were two cans of spray paint. One was blue, and one was green. It was like a bad dream. He wanted to say, *Is that my backpack? How did those get there?* He felt his face turn red. He gulped and tried to speak, but no words came out.

"Spray paint is prohibited in school," Mr. Stevens said icily, "Come with me, Daniel Jones."

The end-of-school bell rang, but for once no one in the class moved. Everyone was too shocked. Daniel Jones was the vandal!

2
MISTRAL

Sara watched in disbelief as Principal Stevens escorted Daniel out. As kids zipped up their backpacks there was excited murmuring in the class. Sara felt everyone's eyes on her. They knew she was Daniel's cousin and best friend. But nobody said anything to her. Did they think she had something to do with the graffiti, too?

She tied and re-tied her shoes until the classroom emptied, and then she went to find her brother.

"Where's Daniel?" asked Jared, who was waiting for her outside.

"He's in the principal's office," Sara said, words rushing out. "They found spray paint in his backpack, but Daniel didn't do it!"

Jared looked shocked. "Well of course he didn't! But who's framing him?"

Sara's eyes widened. She hadn't considered that. Someone must want to make Daniel look guilty. But who?

During a field trip the previous month Sara, together with her cousin and her brother, used their secret code to help the police catch some bank robbers. There was a story about them in the *Browerton Examiner*. Was someone secretly jealous? But then why target Daniel and not her or Jared?

She and her brother went to the main office, where the secretary sat at a desk, on which was a bucket of pens that were decorated like flowers. She gave them a sympathetic smile and waved them towards an empty line of chairs to wait.

Sara remembered these chairs all too well. On her very first day at school she had got into trouble because of the secret code. Luckily, Miss Robinson had given her a second chance. But if Principal Stevens really thought Daniel was guilty of vandalism, he could be kicked out of school!

Sara began counting the floor tiles. Sometimes she liked to count things when she was anxious or upset, and right now she was both. She liked things to make sense, and be fair.

She had counted 382 tiles by the time Daniel finally emerged from the principal's office.

"Mr. Stevens is calling Dad," Daniel said, flopping into a chair. He didn't look surprised to see them. "I told him that the spray cans weren't mine.

Someone must have put them in my backpack."

"Did he believe you?" asked Jared.

"I don't know. I think so. I told him I wouldn't be stupid enough to leave the evidence in my unzipped backpack if I really had spray-painted the wall. And I showed him my hands, so he could see there was no paint on them."

"That was smart," Sara said.

"Also, he asked me a lot of questions about where Mom and Dad work."

"What did the graffiti say?"

"Light lies about Mistral perfume story," Daniel quoted, "Whatever that means. Mr. Stevens didn't say exactly."

"The word 'fume' we saw was just perfume," Sara said, "And 'mist' is for Mistral, the perfume factory."

Mistral Fragrances occupied two brick buildings on the east side of Browerton. This probably meant there were no poisonous fumes coming from the science lab, and no eerie green mist to be found seeping through the hills. Sara was slightly disappointed.

"Hmmm," Jared said, his brow furrowed, "I read something in the paper yesterday about someone stealing from Mistral."

Their conversation was interrupted by Mr. Stevens, who opened his door and stuck his head out.

"Daniel," he said, nodding to Sara and Jared. "If you please." When the principal's door closed behind Daniel, the knot in Sara's stomach tightened. She inspected the floor. Only one small patch of tiles remained to be counted. There were some sections of floor under the desks and cabinets. Sara pondered whether it was worth counting those, too.

When Daniel came out next, he was carrying his backpack. "I'm not suspended exactly," he announced, "I'm on probation or something."

While walking home, Sara and Jared quizzed Daniel about which kids might have tried to frame him. Daniel didn't think he had any enemies. Some people – such as Tom – were not exactly his friends, but they weren't his enemies either.

"But *someone* must be your enemy," Sara persisted.

"If the spray paint has to do with Mistral," Jared said, "then maybe we should be looking for people whose parents work there."

"That's a good idea," Sara agreed. "Isn't Simon Lee in your class, Jared?"

"Who is Simon Lee?" asked Daniel.

"His grandfather owns Mistral," answered Jared, "and yeah, he's in my class."

"But I don't even know him, so why would he pick me to frame?" Daniel said. It was a good point.

"I guess there are lots of kids whose parents work there," Sara said with a frown. "We need to

27

find someone who's your enemy and who also has a Mistral connection."

Daniel just shrugged. "I don't have any enemies," he insisted. "It could be that somebody just wanted to dump the bottles in a hurry, and my backpack was convenient."

When they got to Daniel's house, he and Sara went inside, while Jared headed home. Charles (Daniel's father and Sara's uncle), was usually home when Daniel arrived from school. He was an artist and worked at home. But today it was Daniel's mother (Sara's Aunt Claudine) who greeted them when they walked in. She was a reporter for the *Browerton Examiner* and often worked odd hours. Right now, she was fixing herself a cup of tea in the kitchen.

"How was your day?" she asked, offering them a plate of peach slices.

Daniel knew there was no point holding anything back since the principal had already

28

called his father. "Someone vandalized the wall in the lunch area with spray paint. And they put the spray cans in my backpack, so Principal Stevens thought I did it. But I convinced him it couldn't have been me."

His mother's eyes widened in surprise. "Who put them in your backpack?"

"We don't know."

"Why did Mr. Stevens believe you're innocent if you had the cans?"

"Because we think the graffiti was about stealing at Mistral, and no one in our family works there. Also, I asked him to dust the bottles for fingerprints, so he could see that I never touched them." Daniel started rifling through a pile of newspapers on a corner table.

Sara heard a car door slam, and moments later cousin Isabelle came in with Uncle Charles. Isabelle had recently turned five, and was still in preschool.

"Hi Dair and Sair and Jair," Isabelle greeted Daniel and Sara, waving breezily. She included Jared even though he wasn't there, just because she liked the sound of it. She made them all rhyme with "air."

Daniel and Sara ignored Isabelle, but she didn't notice. She peeled a banana and made funny faces.

Mr. Jones said, "I got a phone call from Mr. Stevens today."

"I already told Mom about it," Daniel interrupted, continuing his search through the newspapers. "I'm looking for the article on Mistral Fragrances."

Mr. Jones raised his eyebrows and looked quizzically at Sara and Daniel.

"Ah, here it is," Daniel said. "The headline is: *Mystery at Mistral.* 'The secretive Mistral Fragrances, Inc., still reeling from the sudden firing of its longtime production manager, Tim McElroy, for safety violations, may have additional demons to battle inside its ranks. According to unconfirmed reports, up to 40 bottles each week of the popular Coralene perfume have been disappearing from the central bottling facility. This is a major expense for the company as Coralene sells for more than $150 for a 2-ounce bottle.'"

"Which rag are you reading?" his mother interrupted.

"It's the *Browerton Light*," Daniel answered.

"The competition!" snorted Daniel's father.

"Typical!" fumed Daniel's mother. "Such shoddy journalism!"

"Why is it bad journalism?" Sara asked.

"They specialize in unconfirmed reports and unnamed sources," Daniel's mother answered. "And lots of sensational phrases like 'demons to battle.' Maybe they think that sells more papers, but it's bad journalism."

"What else does it say?" prompted Sara.

"Mistral founder and Chief Executive Hector

Lee is rumored to be considering stepping down. Possible successors are his oldest son, Oscar Lee, the Chief Designer, and his daughter Penelope Lee, recently promoted to production manager. Mistral sales are up 14% over last year, largely due to the successful introduction of Coralene. Sources inside the company say the thefts began just after Ms. Eva Reynolds was hired as operations manager..." Daniel's voice trailed off as he continued to read.

Eva Reynolds— could that be Kevin's mom? thought Sara. *And I've heard of Penelope Lee before, but where?*

"What else?" Sara persisted, trying to read the paper upside down.

"It's just about the ingredients of Coralene. You know the way people write about perfumes... a shimmering blend of lilies and fermented eels," Daniel joked. "And then at the end it says that members of the Lee family declined to speak to the reporter."

Daniel's father sat next to Daniel and looked over his shoulder at the paper.

"Which reporter?" asked Daniel's mother, her mouth tight.

"It's that Francine Jones again – the one you don't like," Daniel's father answered.

"Why don't you like her?" Daniel asked.

"She writes the most sensational stories. And she never seems to confirm a report with a second source. On top of it all, since we both have the last name Jones, people sometimes confuse us."

"Jones is a boring name," said Isabelle, looking up from her drawing. "When I grow up, I'm going to change my name to Ruby. Isabelle Ruby. Doesn't that sound good?"

"No," said Daniel, "it sounds stupid."

Arguments between Daniel and Isabelle could go on for a good ten minutes. Sara tuned out their conversation and pondered her own buzzing thoughts. How could she find out more about the thefts happening at Mistral? Was Kevin related to Eva Reynolds, the new manager at Mistral? And did the thefts start only after Eva Reynolds was hired?

Was Daniel right that he had no enemies? Was it personal, or was his backpack just chosen at random by someone who needed to get rid of the evidence?

Daniel's conversation with Isabelle shifted to the spray-paint incident. Isabelle was very interested in words painted on tables, and what exactly *vandalized* meant. Isabelle had recently painted on a table by mistake when her paintbrush went off the paper. Perhaps the new word could be applied to that too?

"It's different," Daniel explained. "What you did was an accident, but the paint at school was on purpose."

"The Light lies!" Sara shouted as she jumped up. "That means the Browerton Light!"

Daniel's attention snapped back to Sara. "Wow!", he said, raising his eyebrows at Sara's excitement. Then he got it. "Yes! The graffiti was about this newspaper article!"

"And the offices of the Light are close to school," Sara added. "Maybe whoever wrote the graffiti wanted the reporters to see it."

Sara grabbed the paper, and they both read the article again. It used sensational words, but there were no obvious lies. Sara wrote the names Eva Reynolds and Penelope Lee in her notebook. She put question marks after the names. After some thought, she added the name Francine Jones with a question mark, too. She was going to have to do some careful digging for information.

Now with a new crime to solve, this school year was looking up.

3

LUNCH CLUBS

The mystery of the paint cans was still on Sara's mind as she walked to school with Daniel the next day.

"Earth to Sara!" Daniel said, snapping his fingers in front of her face. "Wake up! I already asked you twice which lunch club you're taking."

"Mosaics," she said, now regretting that she'd told Miss Robinson she would do it.

"I'm trying to find out if we get to eat raw cookie dough in Science of Cooking," Daniel was saying.

"What do you mean, to see if your body becomes a salmonella incubator?" Sara laughed. "Who wants to take a lunch club that will make you sick?"

"Iron stomach," Daniel responded with a shrug, patting his abdomen. "But Anime is also a possibility. It might come in handy for designing video games."

At school, Daniel's friend Jason came running over and gave him a high-five "Daniel, my man! You're not suspended!"

Daniel grinned, "Not yet, but the day is young."

Sara noticed some other kids were pointing and whispering. Daniel was a celebrity once again, but this time he was the wrong kind of celebrity.

37

Sara did not understand how Daniel could be so easy-going about the situation. It wasn't fair that he was being blamed for something he didn't do.

By lunch time, Daniel still hadn't decided which club to go to. In the end, when the bell rang, he murmured to himself "Heads Cooking, tails Anime" and flipped a coin. It landed on tails, so he headed off to Room 109 for the Anime Club.

Sara headed out of the classroom and Kevin ran to catch up with her. She remembered she'd promised to show him how to get to Room 205. Sara was just working up the nerve to ask him about his mother's job at Mistral, but then they arrived.

She looked around curiously. Tables were arranged in a square and kids were already sitting in groups, eating their lunches. Jason and Nayla from Sara's class were there. Sara didn't recognize anyone else.

In the center of the square was a table with objects decorated with many little tiles in pretty patterns. There was a mirror with a floral pattern around it. There was a rectangle that said 4708. Maybe that was somebody's house number. There was a jug and a picture frame.

"Take your seats, folks," said Mrs. Rao.

Sara took a seat next to Kevin.

"In this club, we're going to be learning about mosaics," said the seventh-grade teacher. "Mosaics involve using tiles to make designs, and as an art form they go back well over four thousand years. For the next six weeks we're going to be working on mosaics that are *tessellations*. Who knows what tessellation means?"

The teacher paused and looked at them all expectantly, but the only sound in the room was Jason biting a carrot. Nobody knew the word.

"Tessellation means tiling a flat surface with a geometric shape so that there are no overlaps and no gaps. And who knows what geometric shapes can be used for tessellation?" she asked.

"Squares," said Nayla.

"Triangles," said Kevin.

Sara's mind was already wandering off. This was worse than she thought. She wondered what chemistry the cooking group was learning. She glanced sidelong at Kevin. He was listening intently.

Over the next twenty minutes, Mrs. Rao told the group some history of mosaics, and she turned out the lights for a slideshow. The slides started with old mosaics, from ancient Greece and Rome, and ones from the Byzantine Empire.

The show ended with some very modern pieces, using glass and metal and some weird materials, including medicine pills and trash.

Eventually the lights flicked back on, and the kids finished their lunches while Mrs. Rao finished her explanation.

Sara snapped back to attention when Mrs. Rao asked, "Can someone define a regular polygon?"

Math! thought Sara with relief and put her hand up.

"A regular polygon is a shape where all the sides have the same length, and they have the same angle from one to another," Sara said.

"Very good," said Mrs. Rao, "An example would be a square. And an *irregular polygon* is a shape where the sides are different lengths, or have different angles from one another. An example would be a triangle where one side is longer than the others."

"We're out of time for today. I'm passing out a simple worksheet on tessellating a flat surface – we call it a 'plane,' but I don't mean airplane! – with regular and irregular polygons. You can complete it at home for next time."

Sara put the worksheet neatly in her backpack and stuffed the remains of her lunch in, too. Normally, she would complain to Daniel about lunch club homework, but this sounded like fun.

That evening, Daniel and Isabelle walked over to their cousins' house after dinner. They knew there was leftover cake from the recent birthday of Mr. Felton (their uncle).

"Hi, Aunt Sam. Hi, Uncle Dennis," Isabelle greeted the Feltons. Sara and Jared's parents were still seated at the dinner table, while Jared and Sara cleared the dishes.

"Hi Isabelle. Hi Danny," Mr. Felton said, "Just in time for dessert!" He cut a big slice of cake for Daniel, and a smaller one for Isabelle.

"We heard about yesterday's spray-paint incident," said Mrs. Felton.

"Yeah," said Daniel, "Of course my friends don't think I did it, but everyone else at school... well half of them think I'm cool for being a vandal, and the other half are avoiding me."

"That must be hard," Mrs. Felton said sympathetically.

"He loves the attention!" Jared called from the kitchen.

"True!" Daniel said with a laugh.

He pulled out the paper about orange picking for charity and showed it to his aunt and uncle.

"I bet this kid in my class twenty dollars that I can pick more than him," Daniel bragged, "Sara and Jared are going to be on my team, so could you please sign their permission forms?"

"What does 'more' mean?" Mrs. Felton asked, looking at the paper.

Isabelle looked up, surprised. Even she knew what it meant, and she was only five.

"It means when you have more stuff than someone else," Isabelle said, in a sticky, chocolately sort of voice, eyeing Daniel's slice of cake.

"You know, more!" said Daniel. "More oranges."

"Well, is it more individual pieces of fruit?" asked Mrs. Felton, "or is it more pounds of fruit?" She worked as an engineer, and helped them with their secret code and science fair projects. She always asked interesting questions. "Are you counting the oranges, or are you weighing them to determine the winner?"

"Doesn't it come out to the same thing?" asked Jared, dropping back into his chair and helping himself to a little more cake. "Because more oranges would be heavier."

"Not necessarily," responded Sara, drying her hands on her jeans and sitting down next to her mom. "You could have a few big oranges, or a larger number of small oranges."

"That's right," Mrs. Felton agreed. "Besides, this paper mentions grapefruit too, and the picture shows little tiny things in with the oranges. They're probably cumquats."

"What's a com-cat?" asked Isabelle.

"Cumquats. They're like a tiny little sour orange," answered Mr. Felton, "and if someone picks ten oranges, and someone else picks fifty cumquats, the ten oranges would weigh more than the fifty cumquats. So, the largest *number* of pieces of fruit does not necessarily mean the largest *weight* of fruit."

"Sheesh! This is more complicated than I realized!" Daniel said, drumming his fingers on the table. "Which way am I more likely to win?"

"That depends," answered Mrs. Felton, "We call this type of problem an *optimization* problem. You have something that you want to make as large as possible – or *optimize*. For example, it might be the weight of the fruit. We call that the *objective function*. Suppose the objective function of the fruit picking event is to get the most pounds. And we use the word maximize for making something as large as possible. So, you're trying to maximize an objective function."

"Okay," said Daniel, "so how do you maximize the objective function of getting the most pounds of fruit? Because I really want to win!"

"Well," said Mrs. Felton, "First figure out your *constraints*. The constraints are the *rules* and the *limits* on the situation. For example, maybe you're only allowed to pick for two hours.

Once the event ends and everyone goes home, you guys can't stay behind and keep picking."

"That makes sense," Daniel agreed. "So, once you know the objective function and the constraints, then you can try to figure out a strategy to win."

"What else could be a constraint, besides a time limit?" asked Sara.

"Oh, I don't know," Mrs. Felton answered absent-mindedly, checking a message on her phone, "No climbing trees. Or maybe, squashed fruit doesn't count."

"I think," inserted Mr. Felton, eyeing the cake plates and the crumbs on the table, "that it's time for some *optimization* on this table. It's a mess."

Daniel and Isabelle brought their plates to the kitchen, and then said goodnight and headed home. Jared finished the cleaning-up while Sara started on her homework. She settled down at one end of the long table in the family room and took out her ruler, eraser, colored pens and pencil, and the tessellation worksheet.

At the top of the page, it said "Tessellation = Tiling" and "Have Fun!" in big letters. Sara thought Mrs. Rao had given a slightly more complicated definition of tessellation at the lunch club, something about tiling with a geometric shape and not having any gaps. Sara didn't think it meant just any old tiling, but she didn't feel like checking a dictionary.

The first problem was to draw a tessellation of the flat surface of the paper ("Plane, not airplane" she sang to herself) using regular triangles. She remembered that "regular" meant all the sides were the same length. She used a ruler and measured them carefully to make them perfect. It would have been faster without the ruler and the measuring, but then it would not have been precise, and that would not have suited Sara.

The triangles looked like this:

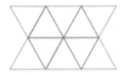

Sara filled in the triangles using alternating colors to make each separate shape stand out. Now it looked like the patterns she'd seen in Mosaics Club.

The next problem was to draw a tessellation using irregular triangles. That meant that the sides were supposed to be different lengths.

Sara used a ruler again and measured precisely.

Then she colored half of them green and admired her work.

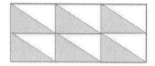

The next problem was to draw squares on a section of the page as if she were putting little mosaic tiles together to form a rectangle. That was of course very easy to do with a ruler.

This time she colored them orange and lavender – one of her favorite color combinations, although her mom said it didn't look good to wear those colors together.

Then came hexagons.

Sara paused. Something felt wrong. Triangles have three sides, and squares have four sides. Hexagons have six sides.

Why skip over pentagons? A pentagon has five sides. It should be three, four, five, *six.*

Sara liked things to be in order, and she wondered if Mrs. Rao had made a mistake and forgotten pentagons. Frowning, she got to work on the hexagons.

It was quite difficult to draw hexagons and make them come out precisely right. After trying for a while with her ruler, and coming out with some lopsided hexagons, Sara decided to print a picture of hexagons from the computer.

She went to the study to collect the printout and discovered that the printer was out of paper. Since these hexagons were not important, Sara loaded the printer with scrap paper that was already printed on one side, instead of using fresh paper.

There was a pile of scrap paper on the desk – pages that Sara had printed the week before, by accident. It was supposed to be a list of her pen pals all on one page, but instead the list had come out with just one name per page – definitely the kind of paper that could be re-used. Sara printed out the image of hexagons. The other side of the page had *Lilja Sturludottir* printed on it. Lilja was one of Sara's Icelandic pen pals.

Sara colored the hexagons in three different colors.

The tessellation looked like this:

Sara cut it out carefully and then taped it to the worksheet. Then she turned to the last sheet. She read: "Trick problem! Try to do this with pentagons!"

Oh good, we're not skipping over pentagons, she thought happily.

She printed some pentagons and cut them out and colored them blue and purple. They had five sides.

They looked like this:

She printed lots of them and cut them out and arranged them next to each other.

It looked like this:

It looked pretty, but there were gaps in between the shapes. Sara tried rearranging the pentagons, but she could not find a way to get rid of the gaps.

After a while, Sara gave up trying and used a yellow marker to color them in.

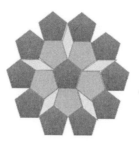

That looks very pretty, Sara thought with satisfaction. *But I don't know why you can tile the plane perfectly – with no gaps – using hexagons, but you can't do it with pentagons.*

Later, in bed, Sara pondered how tidy and organized her hexagons and triangles were, compared to the messiness of real life, with vandalism and theft and people getting framed and almost suspended from school.

When she finally drifted off to sleep, her dreams were filled with pentagons that floated like lily pads on a dark lake. They pushed and heaved and flopped against each other, trying to fit together perfectly. But they couldn't, and the dark water of false accusations and unfairness welled up in the gaps between them.

4

COUNTING M&MS

Kevin stood by Sara's desk. "What did you think of the tessellation homework?" he asked Sara. It was Wednesday, and the end-of-school bell had just rung.

"I liked it." She could feel her ears turning red – something they did when she got nervous.

She desperately tried to think of something else to say. Then she had an inspiration. "Want to get ice cream? The Screamery Creamery has double scoops for the price of one on Wednesdays." If he said yes, then maybe she could figure out a way to ask him about his mom and Mistral Fragrances.

"Sure," said Kevin, smiling.

"I'm coming, too," Daniel said, bounding up behind them to catch a paper airplane thrown by Tariq. He whipped it back to his pal on the other side of the classroom, nearly hitting Miss Robinson.

Sara was annoyed. It would be hard to talk to Kevin about Mistral with Daniel there.

Kevin looked displeased too, but Sara was too preoccupied with her own thoughts to notice, or to wonder why.

Daniel chattered away about his bet with Tom, and his plans to win, as they walked five blocks to the Screamery.

"Happy Wednesday, Sara and Daniel," Mr. Galton greeted them cheerfully. They were regular customers. He nodded pleasantly at Kevin, who hadn't been in the shop before. It was an old-fashioned ice cream parlor that offered root beer floats and banana splits, as well as regular scoops of ice cream.

On the floor at the far end of the counter, a huge plastic cylinder caught Sara's eye. It was about as tall as she was and it was filled with M&M candies. A sign on the counter announced: "GUESS HOW MANY CANDIES – WIN $50 or WEEKLY FREE ICE CREAM FOR A YEAR!!!"

Another sign warned, in smaller letters "Do not touch!! Or you will be disqualified!"

"Wow!" said Daniel, already greedy for the fifty dollars. "I have to win this."

"Free ice cream for a whole year," marveled Kevin.

57

But Daniel promptly said, "Don't be silly, I'd take the cash, not the ice cream."

Daniel went close to the cylinder. He studied it from every angle, trying to come up with the best way to guess the amount.

Daniel started to count the M&Ms. A green one, next to a red, then a blue, then another red, and two browns. Then a yellow, and two more greens.

Meanwhile Sara and Kevin went to the counter.

"I don't know what I want," Sara said, "You go first."

"Are you getting something?" Sara called to Daniel.

"Sssh, I'm counting," he said. Blue, three reds, brown, two yellows, two greens.

"One scoop of strawberry, and one of pistachio, please," said Kevin.

Daniel's count was up to 37, and he was already frustrated. He could see the candies that were right at the edge of the cylinder, and he could partially see the ones right behind them. But those that were any deeper, he couldn't see. Counting what he could see was not going to work.

Daniel wondered how big the container was and whether he could estimate the amount, if he knew its dimensions.

"Here you go," said Mr. Galton, handing the ice cream cone to Kevin.

"Thank you," said Kevin, putting the exact money on the counter.

Daniel wondered how he could measure the container without touching it.

Sara ordered two scoops of Rocky Road ice cream and counted out three dollars and thirty-five cents.

Daniel stood near the cylinder and looked straight at it. Eye level for him was about two inches below the top of the candies. *That's good enough for estimating its height,* he thought.

He pulled a string out of his pocket. *Now I need to know how big around this thing is.*

Daniel realized that he could use the string to measure how far around the cylinder was. Admittedly, the sign said "Do not touch!! Or you will be disqualified!", but Daniel thought he could measure it without actually touching the cylinder. The string would touch the cylinder, but Daniel would not touch it himself.

Daniel was not sure that Mr. Galton would appreciate this careful distinction. He glanced over and saw that the store owner had just finished scooping Sara's ice cream, and that there was no one else in the store.

Mr. Galton gave Sara her ice cream cone.

Daniel looked at Sara. *Maybe I can signal Sara that I need a diversion?* But Sara was not looking at him. The removal of a marshmallow had left a small hole in the side of her ice cream scoop, and she was trying to lick it smooth.

Daniel stretched out his fingers and wiggled them, in a finger-exercising sort of way. Then he flexed his wrist, first one direction, then the other, waiting for Sara to look over.

Sara bit off a huge mouthful of ice cream with nuts and marshmallows, and then she glanced over at Daniel.

Daniel used his hands to signal *finger, finger, finger, fist* at Sara. That was the code for saying that a distraction was needed. Well, at least it used to be. Daniel, Sara and Jared had stopped using the code a month ago, when all that business had happened with the bank robbery, and their secret code had become public knowledge. They hadn't used it since. There wasn't much point in using a secret code that everyone knew about, but he was desperate enough to give it a try.

Sara's eyes widened in surprise. *Daniel needs me to distract Mr. Galton*, Sara thought, with some panic. *What is he up to? What can I do?* She gulped a big breath of air, and the nuts and marshmallow went down the wrong way. Sara coughed violently, accompanied by spluttering and choking noises. She put her hand to her mouth – forgetting that she was still holding the cone – and mashed the ice cream against her cheek.

"Oh, oh!" exclaimed Mr. Galton, "are you OK?"

Kevin grabbed a handful of napkins and held them out, but Sara was coughing too hard to take them.

Daniel quickly squatted down. Holding one end of the string firmly between his right thumb and forefinger he flicked the string hard so that it wrapped around the cylinder and then quickly grabbed the free end of the string with his left hand. He was careful not to break the rules by touching the cylinder – only the string touched it. With his right hand still holding one end of the string in place around the cylinder, Daniel allowed the string to slide between his left thumb and forefinger as he moved his left hand to meet his right hand. When the tips of his forefingers met, he pinched the string hard between his left thumb and forefinger and then let go of the end of the string with his right hand. The length of string dangling from his left hand gave an accurate measurement of the circumference of the cylinder. Carefully holding the string, he stood up.

Sara was still coughing, but recovering, while Kevin dabbed clumsily at her cheek with the napkins. Sara took the napkins from Kevin. Mr. Galton was still hovering near Sara. Seeing that she was okay, Mr. Galton looked over at Daniel.

"Are you having something today, Daniel?" he asked.

"Not today, thank you," Daniel answered as he sauntered out of the parlor. He kept his fingers pinched on the string to mark the spot that would tell him the distance around the cylinder.

Kevin went into the bathroom, while Sara left the parlor holding his ice cream cone as well as her own.

"That was brilliant," Daniel complimented Sara. "I almost thought it was real."

"It *was* real," Sara responded with annoyance. "I was choking. The least you can do is tell me why you needed a distraction."

Daniel held up the string.

His fingers were still pinched on a spot about two feet from the end.

"So what?" asked Sara, "it's a piece of string. You've had it in your pocket for the last week."

"Look at this," he said, "this point on the string tells me the distance around the cylinder with the M&Ms. And I know how tall it is, since it's my eye level plus two inches."

"Oh," said Sara, "if you know the height and the distance around, you can calculate how much space there is inside for the candies!"

"Yup," said Daniel. "Well, I'm going home. You can wait for Kevin."

Daniel took off, with his fingers still pinched on the string.

When Kevin came out of the Screamery, Sara handed back his ice cream. She was pondering how to ask him about his mother. But Kevin spoke first. "Why do you spend so much time with Daniel?"

"He's my cousin," Sara answered.

Kevin looked surprised. But there was something else besides surprise on his face, although he hid it quickly. Sara felt there was something she was missing.

They started walking back towards the school. After a minute of silence, Sara asked, "Why did your family move to Browerton?"

"My mom's job," he answered shortly, taking a bite from his cone.

"Where does she work?"

65

There was silence while Kevin chewed. "At the Mistral perfume factory," Kevin finally responded, not looking at Sara.

"And your dad?"

"He died a few years ago. It's just me and my mom."

Sara felt a rush of sympathy. "I'm so sorry." It seemed inadequate, but she didn't know what else to say.

There was another long minute of silence. They were nearly back at the school, at which point they would start walking in different directions.

At last, Kevin spoke again. "Did Daniel get in trouble for the spray paint?" His voice was carefully neutral.

"No," Sara replied.

A different expression flitted across his face. Was it relief? Or maybe disappointment? Sara couldn't quite tell.

After a moment, Kevin said, "Well, that's good.

Kids shouldn't be blamed for the hateful things their parents do."

Sara was speechless. *Hateful things? What hateful things?*

"Well, I'll see you tomorrow," Kevin said, and started down the side street.

Sara watched him leave, too bewildered to say anything. She couldn't even imagine Aunt Claudine or Uncle Charles doing something hateful. It just wasn't like them.

Sara adjusted her backpack on her shoulders and stared after Kevin.

Somehow in the last two days the placid routine of her life in Browerton had been turned upside down by the trio of mysteries – the perfume theft at Mistral, the graffiti on the wall at school, and Daniel getting framed.

And now Sara added Kevin's bizarre statement about "hateful things" to this growing list of things to worry about. She'd wanted things to become more interesting, but a long worry list had not been exactly what she had in mind.

She took her hair clip off, snapped it closed, and then opened it again. Maybe she should talk to Jared. She repeatedly opened and closed the clip as she slowly walked home, while vague fears floated around the edges of her thoughts. Suddenly the clip snapped into two pieces and at that moment she realized that Kevin and his mom might be at the center of all the mysteries. Sara decided not to say anything to Jared.

When she got home, she discarded the broken pieces of the hair clip and went straight to her room.

5

RANDOM PACKING FRACTION

At Thursday lunch club, Mrs. Rao showed them the main project they would be working on: a mosaic mural, twelve-feet long and six-feet high.

Each kid would get their own section for either a free-form or a geometric design. A border that looked like a braided rope from an ancient Roman floor would snake its way all around the edge.

Mrs. Rao showed the group a collection of one-inch by one-inch square ceramic tiles left over from a house remodeling job. They were one quarter of an inch thick. There weren't nearly enough of them to tile the whole space, so Mrs. Rao asked everyone to check with their parents and bring in additional materials from home.

Sara picked up her pen and nibbled on it. Normally she hated the idea of getting saliva on a writing utensil, but her mind was now so busy that she didn't even notice what she was doing.

She doodled on her paper, making a large question mark shape that had lots of tiny question mark shapes inside it. She crossed her fingers one on top of the other, first on one hand then the other. *Kids shouldn't be blamed for the hateful things their parents do. What exactly did that mean?*

Sara distantly heard Mrs. Rao explain that all sorts of materials could be used for this mosaic

— not just ceramic tiles: thick cardboard boxes, packing materials or foam poster boards would be great. In fact anything that was about one quarter of an inch thick — the thickness of the tiles — would be acceptable, as long as it could be cut into little squares.

After lunch club Sara followed Kevin out of the classroom, and then pulled him into an empty hallway.

"What did you mean yesterday?" she blurted out. "What hateful thing did Daniel's parents do?"

Kevin looked down at his hands. Then he looked up, his eyes flashing angrily.

"His mom wrote that article about Mistral! She said the stealing started after Eva Reynolds was hired," Kevin answered angrily, "and Eva Reynolds is my mom."

"Oh no!" said Sara, "Daniel's mom didn't write that."

"Huh?" Kevin blurted.

"That was Francine Jones, in the *Browerton Light*. My aunt is Claudine Jones, and she writes for the *Browerton Examiner*. Daniel's family are not related to Francine Jones."

"Oooh!" Kevin drew in his breath sharply. His face went a bit red and he turned slightly away from Sara, crossing his arms in front of him, then uncrossing them, while avoiding her gaze. "I didn't..." he began, but then stopped abruptly.

"It was you, wasn't it!" Sara declared fiercely, pointing an accusatory finger at him and nearly jabbing him in the chest. Her whole body had suddenly tensed, like a leopard about to attack. "You put the spray paint in Daniel's backpack!"

Kevin pushed Sara's arm away. His face was angry and bitter.

"My mom was crying when she read that newspaper story! She didn't do anything... she wouldn't steal, but now people think she did it."

72

Sara started to turn away, but Kevin grabbed her arm and swung her around to face him.

"You have to believe me. I didn't spray-paint the wall; I just saw those cans and stuck them in Daniel's backpack." Kevin sounded desperate. "I don't want to have to move again."

Before Sara could say anything, he turned and ran towards their classroom.

Sara stood still and realized that she was biting her lip so hard it hurt. *Even if his mom is innocent, what Kevin did was wrong,* Sara thought. *Should I tell one of the teachers?*

When the bell rang for the end of school, the decision about whether to tell Daniel, Jared, or a teacher was still swirling around in her head. She even thought about calling her Uncle George for advice. Although Uncle George lived far away, he always knew how to handle tricky situations.

Kevin caught her eye from across the room. Sara read the question on his face: *Are you going to tell?*

And suddenly, without talking to anyone, she knew that she wasn't going to. She didn't know if it was because she felt sorry for him because his dad had died, or because of his worry for his mom, or for some other reason. She just knew that she wasn't going to tell.

She gave him a tiny smile and a shake of her head. *No.*

That evening after dinner, Daniel came over to see what Sara's mom might know about how many M&M candies could be packed in a container. Isabelle came too, because any discussion about candy was of interest to her. Daniel tried to tell her that there weren't going to be any actual M&Ms at Aunt Sam's house, but she wasn't buying it.

"What measurements do you have?" Mrs. Felton asked.

"The cylinder was 61 inches tall," began Daniel, "and the circumference was 33 inches."

"What is a circum fence?" asked Isabelle.

"Cir-cum-fer-ence," Mrs. Felton said slowly. "it's not related to a fence. It's the distance to go around a circle. Or in this case, the distance to go around a cylinder."

She took a sheet of paper and drew a circle. "If you go straight across a circle, that distance is called the diameter," she said, "And if you go around the circle, that distance is called the circumference."

She wrote *diameter* and *circumference* on the paper.

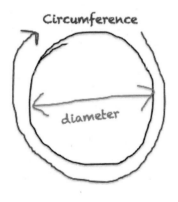

"The circumf'rence of my glass is ten fingers!" said Isabelle, holding her glass up carefully with two hands.

"That's the idea," her aunt said with a smile, "but not exactly."

Mrs. Felton got a tape measure and measured the distance around the glass. "See, the circumference is four and a half inches. But that is just about ten fingers."

"To get the area of the circle," Daniel continued, "you have to know that area equals circumference squared divided by about 12.6."

Sara wrote on the paper:

Cylinder height = 61 inches,
Circumference = 33 inches,
Area = Circumference squared / 12.6
=33 x 33 / 12.6
= 86.4 inches square

She tapped on her calculator and then wrote down:

Cylinder volume = Height x Area
= 61 x 86.4 = 5,270 cubic inches

"There you go," Sara said, sounding pleased with herself, "the area of the circle is about 87 square inches, and the volume of the entire cylinder is 5,270 cubic inches."

"5,270?" Isabelle said, "That's loud!"

Daniel laughed. "No, not that kind of volume! Here *volume* means how much space there is inside the cylinder. If we know how much space there is inside the container, and we know how much space one M&M takes up, then I can figure out how many M&Ms are inside the cylinder and win fifty dollars!"

"It's not a simple calculation though," said his aunt. "First of all, if you were to put the M&Ms in the cylinder very carefully, putting one as close as possible to the next one, there would still be some gaps in between them."

"Why would there be gaps?" asked Isabelle, "I bet I could put them in perfectly, if I tried."

"Even if you put them in perfectly," said Mrs. Felton, "there would still be gaps."

She reached for the paper and started drawing little circles.

"Imagine these circles are M&Ms," she said, "and I place them right next to each other like this. You can see there are some little gaps between the circles."

Mrs. Felton scribbled a bit with a green pencil in each of the gaps.

Then her picture looked like this:

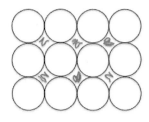

"If I take some of the rows of M&Ms and slide them over, I can then push them a bit closer together," she explained, "but there are still gaps."

She drew the circles over again, but this time the alternate rows were staggered, so the circles sat more closely together.

Isabelle inspected the picture closely. "There are still some tiny gaps," she declared.

"Yes," Mrs. Felton agreed, "but they are smaller than before. This is what is called *close packing*. This is as close together as you can put circles."

She drew a hexagon in red neatly on top of the circles:

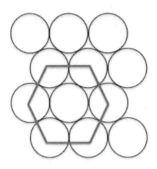

"Each circle is surrounded by six other circles in a perfect regular hexagon," she said, "so this is called *hexagonal* packing."

"They look like flower petals around the middle of the flower!" exclaimed Isabelle.

"So how do we figure this out?" asked Daniel. "We can't just divide the volume of the cylinder by the volume of one M&M and say that is the number of M&Ms."

"No, you can't," agreed Mrs. Felton. "And actually it's worse than that, because the candies are not close packed inside the cylinder. They are just dropped in, and they end up wherever they end up. It's random."

"But then it's hopeless," sighed Daniel, slumping down in his chair. "If it's random, I can't calculate how many there are, so I can't win!"

"Well, since it's random, you can't calculate *exactly* how many there are," Mrs. Felton said. "But you can calculate a very good guess. What we need is something called the *random packing fraction.*"

"What's that?" asked Jared, who was only now tuning in to the conversation.

"It's the fraction of space that is occupied by objects of the same shape and size if you just drop them in to a container. When you do that, they get packed pretty close together without being truly lined up," Mrs. Felton answered.

"What's a fraction of space?" asked Isabelle.

"It's math that someone has already worked out

for us," said Daniel. He quickly typed "random packing fraction" into the search bar on his laptop. A long list of entries popped up on his screen. He clicked on the first one. Jared looked over his shoulder.

"It says 64%" Daniel said. "Does that mean 64% of the space is filled by the candies?"

"That's the random packing fraction for *spheres*," said Jared, who was reading fast, "like perfectly round balls. But M&Ms aren't exactly balls. They're a bit flattened."

"You could add M&M to your search," Sara suggested.

Daniel scoffed, "I doubt that anyone has calculated random packing fractions for candies."

But he typed in M&M as an additional search term, just in case.

To everyone's surprise, another long list of search entries popped up.

"Wow, there's lots of packing fractions worked

out for lots of candies," Daniel marveled, "it's 68% for M&Ms."

Mrs. Felton looked over his shoulder and read the screen. "That's right," she agreed, "When you pour them in a jar, M&Ms do occupy a bit more of the space than spherical candies do."

Daniel wrote on his paper:

Random Packing Fraction = 0.68

He read from the online list that the volume of one M&M candy is 0.636 cubic centimeters, so he added to his paper.

1 M&M = 0.636 cubic centimeters

Sara handed him her paper and he copied the volume from that.

> Volume of cylinder
> = 5,270 cubic inches
> 5,270 x 16.3871
> = 86,360 cubic centimeters

"If the whole space could be filled with candies," said Daniel, "then the number of candies would be just the volume of the whole cylinder divided by the volume of one candy."

He wrote down:

> Number of candies
> (if whole space filled)
> = cylinder volume / candy volume
> = 86,360 / 0.636 = 135,786!!!

"Wow, that is a large number," exclaimed Sara.

"Yes," agreed Daniel, "but we still have to adjust it by the random packing fraction, because the candies don't fill the whole space."

He added the final line:

> Number of actual M&Ms
> = 135,786 x Random Packing Fraction
> = 135,786 x 0.68 = 92,334!!!

"Ninety-two thousand, three hundred and thirty-four!" Daniel exclaimed, and Sara said "That's still a huge number."

"I'm sure I'll win!" said Daniel, drumming his hands on the table. "Sara, tomorrow let's go to the parlor and drop off my winning answer." In a low voice he said, "And I guess I owe you an ice cream because you helped with the diversion."

He grinned happily at his cousin, but Sara felt like a traitor. She knew who'd framed him, but she couldn't tell him. If Daniel found out what Kevin had done and that she knew, would he forgive her?

6
OPTIMIZING TOYS AND ORANGES

On Friday morning Daniel and Jared helped Sara carry two large cardboard boxes and the foam board from Jared's old science fair project to school. It was all material for the Mosaics Club.

It wasn't an official lunch club day, but anyone who wanted to start working on mosaic tiles was allowed to. During lunch, Daniel, Sara and Kevin sat with Jason and Nayla and cut out one-inch by one-inch squares of board.

Daniel was in the Anime Club, not the Mosaic Club, but since it wasn't an official lunch club day he just tagged along.

Sara almost wished he hadn't come. Every time she looked at Daniel she felt like she had a lead ball in her stomach. Sara had never kept information from Daniel before, and she still didn't know if she believed Kevin was innocent as far as the spray painting was concerned. But after a while she relaxed and concentrated on cutting out squares.

Nayla had brought in dozens of foam rectangles to cut. They were just the right thickness – a quarter of an inch.

Sara admired the color, which was a very bright lime green. And foam was easy to cut.

"Where did you get these?" Sara asked.

"I found them in a dumpster by my apartment. I think maybe they're packing material."

Sara thought it was pretty disgusting to dig something out of a dumpster. But she didn't say anything because she didn't want to hurt Nayla's feelings. Nevertheless, Sara was careful not to touch the green foam rectangles in case of germs.

The science fair board was large – four feet tall – so you could cut hundreds of one-inch squares out of it. Kevin struggled to fit the scissors in, so Daniel leaned over and held an end to make it easier for him.

"Thanks," Kevin mumbled.

"Sure!" Daniel said with his usual friendliness. "Hey, in Anime Club we're drawing our own avatars for video games. What would yours be?"

"Octopus," Kevin answered, and Daniel raised an eyebrow. "Useful to have eight arms," Kevin explained, and they started talking enthusiastically about their favorite characters.

Sara didn't say anything. She was feeling resentful. Here were Daniel and Kevin chatting away like old friends, and Kevin seemed to be perfectly fine with it. But Sara was not perfectly fine. She was forced to keep his secret.

Her scissors got stuck in the stiff poster board, and she angrily jerked them free, making a small cut on her left hand.

"Ouch," Sara grunted, as a drop of blood appeared on her finger.

Kevin fished a napkin from his pocket and held it out, but Sara just scowled and muttered "No, thanks."

She wiped her finger on her jeans and stopped cutting altogether.

Kevin watched Sara uneasily, trying to pay attention to her, the cutting project, and Daniel's conversation at the same time.

After lunch club, they walked back to class. Daniel was still chattering on about his character.

"I need to apologize to you," Kevin said suddenly, interrupting him.

"Huh? What for?"

"It was me. Uh, I put the spray paint in your backpack." He took a step backwards in case Daniel decided to hit him.

Daniel just blinked at him in confusion.

"Why?"

"Because I thought your mom wrote that mean article about my mom and the factory thefts," Kevin said. "But Sara told me it wasn't your mom who wrote it."

"No, she's a real journalist," Daniel responded, "She always does her research and writes fair stories."

"I'm really sorry," Kevin said. "I think someone is trying to make it look like my mom is stealing the perfume."

"Wow," said Daniel. "That's awful."

"You're not mad?" asked Kevin, incredulously.

"No," responded Daniel, "I mean, I didn't get in any major trouble, so it's okay." He shrugged. "And I guess I'm glad to know I don't have an enemy. I didn't think I did, but you never know."

Kevin stuck out his hand and Daniel shook it.

At that, Sara felt as though a huge weight had been lifted from her shoulders, and her resentment fell away.

"Have they caught the person stealing the perfume yet?" Daniel asked. Kevin looked glum and shook his head. "I wish there was something I could do. My mom is so worried. She's sure everyone thinks she's doing it."

Just before the final bell rang, Miss Robinson asked, "Who is planning to come to the orange picking charity event?"

About half the class raised their hands, and Miss Robinson looked pleased.

"That's great," she said. "I'm going to have two boxes for each person to fill."

After the bell rang, Daniel went up to Miss Robinson to ask a quick question. Kevin gave Sara a wave, and she called out to him, "Want to come over?"

He lit up with a smile. "Really? Yeah!"

Daniel caught up with them. They headed to his house first to see if there were any good snacks to be had. A few slices of cherry pie were left in a pie tin on the table. Isabelle was there, standing on a chair by the counter. She had a smear of cherry pie filling on her cheek. In front of her the KitchenAid mixer was whirring around at full speed.

"Are you allowed to do that?" Sara demanded, serving herself some pie. She didn't think Aunt Claudine and Uncle Charles would permit Isabelle to use the mixer.

"What are you making?" asked Daniel at the same time, wondering why the batter wasn't splattering out of the bowl at that speed.

"I'm not making anything," Isabelle responded haughtily, looking down at them from the chair height. "I'm giving Squirrel a ride. Who are you?" she asked Kevin.

"This is Kevin," said Sara.

Isabelle smiled at Kevin. She liked having an audience. She switched the mixer speed from 12 down to 2. They could see the small brown creature attached to the beater with a rubber band.

"He's getting dizzy," announced Isabelle, turning the mixer off and detaching the stuffed animal. "Now he wants to go in the fridge and chill." She opened the fridge and popped Squirrel in.

"Sisters!" Daniel said with a sigh.

"I wish I had one," Kevin said wistfully.

They ate pie, but Sara's mind was stuck on the mixer. *Who knows where that toy has been?* she thought to herself. She put the bowl and beater in the sink and filled the bowl with soapy water.

They decided to stay at Daniel's house and play a video game. Then Kevin had to head home, and Sara decided she'd better leave, too.

"Do you think your mom is home yet?" Daniel asked, "It might be good if she's around when we're trying to figure out the optimization."

"Probably not yet," said Sara, "Come over for dinner." And off she went.

That evening, Daniel and Isabelle showed up for spaghetti night. Isabelle loved slurping the noodles. Daniel mainly wanted to figure out some orange packing strategies.

"Can we borrow your bucket of tennis balls?" Daniel addressed himself to his aunt, "We want to figure out some optimization strategies for orange packing."

"I have an optization problem too," announced Isabelle.

Mrs. Felton smiled. "Let's hear it," she said to

Isabelle, "but the word is op-ti-mi-za-tion, not op-ti-za-tion."

"Well," said Isabelle, looking around to make sure that Jared was listening too, "My teacher said she wanted to see who could pick up the most toys the fastest. And I asked her if *most toys* wins or if *fastest* wins. Cuz those are different things."

"You're absolutely right," said Mrs. Felton approvingly, "that's not a well-defined optimization problem. One doesn't know what exactly to try to maximize there – the number of toys, or the speed, or some combination."

"So, what happened?" Jared prompted.

"She said forget about fast, that *most toys* would win," Isabelle held out her arms wide, as if to show a lot of toys. "So, I picked up five, and Alicia went fast and got six, and all the other kids got some, and I lost because I only got five."

"Well, why didn't you just keep on going and get more than five?" asked Mrs. Felton.

"There weren't any more!" Isabelle answered in a mournful voice, "They were all picked up."

"Oh, I see," said Mrs. Felton, "there just weren't enough toys. So even though the teacher said that going fast didn't matter, it really *did* matter. Only the number of toys was in the objective function, but you still had to go fast or else you couldn't pick up a large number."

Isabelle looked rather accusingly at her aunt, "Being fast wasn't in the jective function."

"*Ob*-jective function," Mrs. Felton corrected, "And yes, this is a situation where speed was not *explicitly* part of the objective function being maximized. That means it's not *directly* part of the objective function. The objective function was just the number of toys, which is all you were trying to maximize. But speed is still *implicitly* part of the objective function. That means it's hidden in there, because the number of toys you can pick up still depends on the speed."

Isabelle pondered this explanation for a moment, and then scowled. "Alicia won," she said, and went back to slurping noodles.

Mrs. Felton sighed and told Daniel that the tennis balls were in the garage.

In the family room, with some boxes and two large buckets of tennis balls, Daniel shared the orange picking information with Jared. "Miss Robinson said she'd give two boxes per person. So, the three of us will have six boxes. I asked how big, and she said two feet by two feet by one and a half, or a little more."

"So, the question is," said Sara, "now we know the main constraint is that we only have six boxes, how do we win the bet?"

There was silence for a moment, while they all thought this over. Then Jared picked up a bucket of balls and dumped them into a box. He tried the same thing with the second bucket, but most of those balls didn't fit and bounced and rolled all over the floor.

"Humph," said Daniel, scurrying to collect the scattered balls, "this does not feel like optimization."

Sara took some balls out of the box and put them back in the bucket. She adjusted the positions of the rest of the balls, moving them around to make them fit closer together.

Jared picked up his guitar and strummed some chords. Daniel lay down flat next to the couch and reached as far as he could underneath to collect the stray balls. He got the yardstick out of the broom closet to knock the last ones out. When Daniel returned to the box, Sara had made a layer of balls that looked like this:

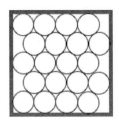

As Daniel watched, she started another layer on top by placing a ball so it nestled down into the dip formed by the three balls below it:

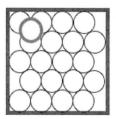

Soon her second layer started to look like this:

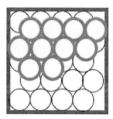

Each ball sat tightly up against its neighbors and was offset from the ones below.

Mrs. Felton walked in, carrying two errant balls that had rolled all the way into the kitchen. She looked into the box.

"Cool," she said, "I think that packing is called an HCP configuration."

Everyone looked at her blankly. "HCP stands for Hexagonal Close Packing," Mrs. Felton continued, "Along with something called the face-centered cubic packing, it's the tightest packing you can manage in three-dimensional space."

"But what about the wasted space at the edge of the box?" asked Daniel.

"Well," she said, "in the real world they would pack some filler material around there so things wouldn't move. You could use some crumpled newspaper."

Mrs. Felton left the room, adding over her shoulder "Take the *Browerton Light* – it does really well as packing material."

This was not a very satisfactory answer. None of them moved to get any newspaper. It didn't seem like crumpled paper packed into the edges of the box would help the optimization.

Sara took some colored pencils and started drawing a box with circles. She labeled the box neatly with the word "Box" and added a second layer of circles.

Then Jared suggested, "How about if we pop some cumquats in there?"

Sara clapped her hands with delight. She took an orange pencil and added seven cumquats to her picture.

It looked like this:

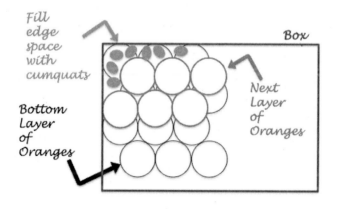

"That looks good," said Daniel, "and then we don't have to check with Tom whether it's number of fruits or weight of fruit that's in the objective function."

"Yeah," Sara agreed, "lots of cumquats around the edge would make the *number* high, and close packing of everything in the box would make the *weight* high."

"So, we'd win either way," Jared concluded with satisfaction, looking up from his guitar.

They put the balls back in the buckets, and Sara folded her picture and tucked it away in her pocket. Mrs. Felton came back in with one last ball.

She asked, "Do any of you remember my friend Penelope Lee?"

Sara jumped up. That name was important. It was from the newspaper article. Was Penelope Lee her mother's friend?

"Aren't her parents the owners of Mistral?" asked Jared, shooting a look at his sister.

"Yes, that's right" their mother replied. "Penelope works there, and her brother does too. Well, because of the thefts, they're thinking of putting in an RFID system at the factory."

"What's that?" asked Daniel.

"RFID stands for Radio Frequency IDentification," answered Mrs. Felton. "Tiny little electronic devices can be attached to merchandise — like the perfume containers. The devices transmit radio signals and let you know where they are.

So, basically, Mistral could attach one of these RFID devices to each individual perfume bottle, and it would transmit where exactly each bottle is as it gets moved around. You can keep track of all the bottles in the warehouse. And you could even see where and when each bottle exits the warehouse. It would make them harder to steal."

"Cool," said Sara. *Maybe this will help Kevin's mom!*

"Penelope wants my advice, and I thought a perfume factory would be interesting for you to see, too, so I asked if I could bring you kids along. Do any of you want to go with me tomorrow to visit Mistral?"

"Yes!" said Jared, Daniel and Sara all at the same time.

"Jinx," Daniel cried. "You both owe me a soda!"

Sara rolled her eyes at him.

Ignoring the exchange, Mrs. Felton grinned at their enthusiasm, "Nine sharp tomorrow. No chance to sleep in."

It was worth having to set her alarm on the weekend, thought Sara. A tour of a factory was bound to be interesting, and snooping around a factory that had a thief was going to be even more interesting.

7
INSIDE THE FACTORY

Saturday morning came, cloudy and cold. After breakfast Daniel, Jared and Sara piled into the minivan with Mrs. Felton.

She had just turned on the engine when her phone chirped.

"Hold on," she exclaimed, picking up the

phone, "It's Penelope." Mrs. Felton swiped the phone and read the message.

"Well, she's going to be a little bit late, but she says we should still come. Her sister-in-law is there now and can meet us."

"How do you know Penelope Lee?" asked Daniel.

"We went to college together," Mrs. Felton said. "We've been friends for a long time, and I know this situation is weighing on her. So, I want to help if I can."

They passed Sara's favorite bookstore which was right next to her favorite donut place. But Sara was eager to get to Mistral, so she did not beg her mom to stop.

The Mistral site looked neither glamorous nor sinister. On one side of the street there was a long low building that went on for several blocks. On the other side was a parking lot and a four-story brick building with big glass doors.

The sign said "Mistral" in curvy letters, and a pleasant little garden with purple and white flowers surrounded the sign. Everything looked quite ordinary.

"Take that umbrella," suggested Mrs. Felton before they exited the van, "I think it might be raining by the time we're done."

A woman came out of the glass doors to meet them. She was wearing blue jeans and a white sweatshirt with the Mistral logo in purple across the front.

"Hello, welcome to Mistral! I'm Valerie Abbott."

"Thanks for meeting us here" said Mrs. Felton, "We've met once before, I think, at Penelope's house."

"Yes, indeed," Ms. Abbott beamed, and then, turning to the others, she said, "You ready for a tour?"

Mrs. Felton introduced Jared and Sara and Daniel.

"Let's start on this side of the street," Ms. Abbott suggested, "This is where we have our research and development labs, and the corporate offices."

The guard at the desk said good morning to them and handed a clipboard to Ms. Abbott. She wrote down their names on the page, in the space where it said *Visitors.*

"The first two floors have the labs," Ms. Abbott said, "and then upstairs we have the marketing department and so forth. Upstairs is kind of boring, but I think you might like the labs."

They walked down a long hallway, and then Ms. Abbott used a card key attached to her belt to unlock a set of double doors.

She ushered them into a large room that looked like the best mad-scientist chemistry lab Sara had ever seen.

Hundreds and hundreds of small labeled bottles stood in tall racks. Next to them, glass beakers filled with liquids of different colors bubbled and foamed. Pipes snaked along the ceiling and down the walls, connecting with shiny brass vats.

On the sides of the vats were control panels studded with knobs and lights that blinked. Gleaming white tables stood in the center of the room, covered with mysterious equipment that whirred and flashed. Against the wall stood even more mysterious equipment that just sat there and didn't let on what it was for.

Sara wanted to know what everything did, and Ms. Abbott generously answered all her questions.

Centrifuges were machines that could spin bottles of liquids around very, very fast, so that the denser particles in the liquid would separate from the less dense bits. *Distillation* involved heating a liquid so that the water would evaporate away, leaving behind whatever things didn't boil away. When she explained how perfume is made, Jared and Daniel started to look bored.

"Valerie, Sara will keep you here all day if you let her," said Mrs. Felton.

Ms. Abbott smiled at Sara and said, "I don't mind the questions," and finished explaining about essential oils.

"Is this where the perfume bottles are getting stolen from?" Jared asked when there was a pause.

"No. This is where we develop new products. The manufacturing is all on the other side of the street."

"What's your theory about the stealing?" asked Daniel.

"Daniel!" said his aunt disapprovingly, "I'm sure Valerie can't discuss it."

Ms. Abbott pursed her lips and blew out a long breath.

"I don't know, Daniel. I don't even have a theory. But an RFID system should solve the problem. Let's go across the street to see where the RFID would be used. Shall we?"

They left the remarkable chemistry lab, with all its intriguing equipment, and walked across the street. It was beginning to rain.

Ms. Abbott held the door for them.

The security guard looked bored. "Good morning, Ms. Abbott," he said, holding out a clipboard.

"Here I need *you* to sign in," said Ms. Abbott, giving the clipboard to Mrs. Felton.

The guard pressed a button to let them through the next door.

"Everything you carry out has to pass through this," Ms. Abbott said, gesturing to the X-ray machine next to the guard's station.

Mrs. Felton glanced at the X-ray machine and made a note on her tablet.

They went down a corridor, and Daniel stopped for a moment to read a poster on the wall. The others went around a corner, not noticing that Daniel had fallen behind.

"What the hell are you doing here?" said an angry voice, and Daniel looked up to see a tall, bearded man glaring at him, "Who are you?"

"I'm Daniel," Daniel managed to answer, "uh, Daniel Jones. I'm here with my aunt."

"Who is she? Where is she?" the man demanded, but at that moment Ms. Abbott popped back around the corner, followed by Mrs. Felton and the others.

"It's all right, Mr. Warren," Ms. Abbott said hurriedly, "he's with me."

Mr. Warren looked them over. He clearly did not think it was all right.

"Why are they here?" he asked.

"This is Samantha Felton," responded Ms. Abbott, "she's an engineer, and Penelope asked for her advice on an RFID system."

"RFID," Mr. Warren grunted, "stupid waste of money, if you ask me. This place can't afford fancy gizmos. Everyone knows they don't work."

"They do work," Mrs. Felton began, but Mr. Warren scowled at them and walked away, growling over his shoulder "Just stay out of the restricted areas."

Jared, Sara and Daniel looked at each other in surprise. They weren't used to this kind of rudeness.

"Who is he?" Mrs. Felton asked Ms. Abbott, "and why is he here on a Saturday?"

"Mr. Warren is the shipping manager," said Ms. Abbott, "and I'm not really sure why he's here right now, probably just catching up on paperwork."

"What are the restricted areas?" asked Sara, hoping to go there.

Ms. Abbott led them down another hallway.

"Well, it's all restricted here," she answered, "one level or another of restricted access. That's why the guard at the front has to buzz you in. Our perfumes are made with very secret formulas. We can't let just anyone have access."

They saw a room where various liquids in big vats were waiting to be bottled. Mrs. Felton made some notes on her tablet.

After the bottling room, they saw machines for attaching labels. Mrs. Felton made some more notes. The machinery was shut down because it was the weekend.

It would be interesting to watch it when it was all running. Sara hoped they might be able to come back during the week, when everything was whirring along at full speed.

Sara and Jared and Daniel lingered to look at the machines.

"Do you think that Mr. Warren might be the thief?" Daniel said softly to Sara.

Mrs. Felton was at the other end of the large room, having a quiet discussion with Ms. Abbott.

"I don't know. I suppose if he's the shipping manager, he has lots of chances to take bottles," Sara answered.

"But you saw the X-ray machine at the entrance," Jared put in, "You can't just walk out of this building carrying stuff."

"Well," said Daniel, "I don't like him, and he definitely didn't like us."

They left the labeling room and walked down a flight of stairs to another big room with several hallways leading off from it. Part of the floor was lower down, with a few steps leading to it. Boxes were stacked in piles in one part of the room. A forklift was parked near them. There were also a couple of machines, but Daniel couldn't figure out their purpose.

A conveyor belt led from another room through an opening in the wall into one side of this room. The belt was not moving. Mrs. Felton seemed interested in it and wrote something in her notepad.

Half of one wall had some cabinets, and a pegboard with some tools. Sara saw a drill and some screwdrivers and wrenches. She wondered if the tools were meant for fixing the conveyor belt or the machines if they broke down.

Mr. Warren stood there, putting some papers in a cabinet. He did not look happy to see them.

"This is where the shipping boxes go out," said Ms. Abbott, "the last stop before the loading dock." She picked up a rectangular box of thick cardboard. It was about five inches long. "This is the type of box we use for Coralene. It holds twenty bottles, four rows with five bottles each."

Mrs. Felton measured the box and made a note.

Ms. Abbott walked over to the row of cabinets and opened a drawer. Mr. Warren continued standing there, with a sour expression. Ms. Abbott picked up a small cylindrical box of thin white cardboard. It was printed with a spray of lavender flowers, circling all the way around. She lifted a bottle out of the box. "This is a Coralene bottle," she explained, "This one is empty, obviously.

There's metal in the cap. It shows up quite clearly on the X-ray machine, so it can't be taken out through the main door without us knowing."

"It's a very pretty box," said Sara, admiringly.

"You can have it," said Ms. Abbott with a smile, handing Sara the little flower-covered cylinder of cardboard. "This is how it looks when it is sold in stores. The other box is just for shipping."

Ms. Abbott gave one of the boxes to Daniel, and offered one to Jared too, but he shook his head.

"No bottle breakage?" Mrs. Felton asked.

"No, almost never," said Ms. Abbott. "Not unless you drop the box. But we put in a couple pieces of quarter-inch padding to make sure."

Daniel was starting to get a bit bored.

The chemistry lab had been more interesting. He walked over to the edge of the stairs and looked down at the lower area. More boxes and crates.

Daniel pulled out his phone and started playing MicroBat. His game was interrupted by a text from Sara across the room. *Stay alert! Look for clues!* it said.

Sara was right; he should stay focused on how the bottles could be getting stolen. On the little screen, his MicroBat careened into the cave wall.

Daniel looked over the room. *I wonder if they drive the forklift out of here? Maybe you could hide a few bottles in the seat cushion.*

Meanwhile Sara looked around the room. She peered down one of the hallways. It had corkboards on the walls, with lots of papers pinned to them. There were some closed doors along the side, and an emergency exit at the end – nothing of obvious interest.

Sara looked down the other hallway. It was more dimly lit. About twenty feet away there was something green on the floor. *Where have I seen that before?* Sara thought.

She took a step down the hall.

"Stop! You can't go there," Mr. Warren barked loudly. Sara wheeled around and took a step back into the main room.

Mr. Warren was clearly annoyed.

"Ms. Abbott," he called across the room to where Ms. Abbott and Mrs. Felton were talking, "Don't you think your visitors have been here long enough?"

Sara looked back down the hallway. *I've definitely seen that before*, she thought.

"We're almost finished, Mr. Warren," said Ms. Abbott. "Five minutes."

Sara caught Daniel's eye. She signaled *finger, finger, finger, fist* to him. Jared saw it too. *A diversion!* thought Daniel, startled, *what is Sara planning now?*

Daniel glanced down. *What could he do?* He was at the edge of the stairs. He put his cell phone in his pocket so it wouldn't hit the floor. He started to take a step backwards, flailed his foot around in the air for a moment, and then pretended to fall down the three stairs onto the lower section of the room. The little Coralene box clattered out of his hand and down the three stairs.

"Watch out," yelled Jared, too late to be of any use. Mrs. Felton started running towards Daniel, calling out "Are you okay?"

All eyes were on Daniel. All eyes, that is, except for Sara's.

She zipped down the hallway towards the green thing on the floor. There it was, a little lime-green rectangle made of foam. She'd seen something like it just recently, but where?

She snatched it off the floor, stuffed it in her pocket, and zipped back to the main room.

Daniel was trying to pick himself up, not entirely successfully.

Jared was yelling "Oh my God, are you okay?" while flailing his arms around, hoping that nobody was aware that Sara had disappeared.

"My dearest cousin," said Jared loudly, "here, let me get your box." He picked up the Coralene box and vigorously wiped it off, although there was nothing on it.

Mrs. Felton gave Jared a strange look.

Ms. Abbott appeared very worried, and Daniel wondered momentarily how much to play things up. But then Daniel saw that Sara had returned, so he said, "I'm okay, no really, I'm fine" and then stood up and brushed himself down.

Mr. Warren muttered something about *darned nuisance* and *children* and *liability*. Daniel and Jared could not catch all of his words, but they got the general drift.

"I think I've got the idea of what's needed here," said Mrs. Felton hurriedly, looking suspiciously at her offspring and nephew. "Thank you so much, Valerie, for giving us the tour."

"Yes, thank you!" Sara, Jared and Daniel echoed politely.

Ms. Abbott escorted them to the front of the building, and Mrs. Felton hastily scribbled 10:30 on the clipboard for their departure time.

And with one last "You're sure you're all right, dear?" and "Penelope will be so sorry to have missed you" from Ms. Abbott, and "I'll be in touch with Penelope, thank you again," from Mrs. Felton, they piled back into the minivan.

8

STEALING PERFUME

"All right, folks," said Mrs. Felton, once the minivan was safely down the street from Mistral, "what was all that back there?"

"What was what?" asked Jared, innocently.

"You know," retorted Mrs. Felton, "that whole 'My dear cousin' business."

Daniel, Sara and Jared looked at one another.

"What?" protested Jared. "Can't I be concerned about my dear cousin Daniel?"

Mrs. Felton sighed and turned on the radio.

At home, Mr. Felton was starting to make lunch. "What toppings do you want?" he asked. After the pizza toppings were sorted out, Jared, Sara and Daniel went to Jared's room and closed the door.

"So, what's going on?" asked Daniel, "what was so important that I had to fake falling down the stairs?"

"Yeah," Jared chimed in, "And what's the idea of resurrecting the secret code? I thought we were done with that."

"I thought we were done too," said Sara, "but, you know, these situations keep coming up."

"Well," persisted Jared, "why did you need the diversion?"

"This," responded Sara, pulling out the rectangle of lime-green foam.

"Isn't that the same stuff that Nayla brought to school from a dumpster?" asked Daniel.

"Exactly," answered Sara, "Why is a big stack of this fancy packing material from Mistral showing up in a dumpster near Nayla's house?"

They sat and pondered the rectangle of green foam. Jared got out a ruler and measured it.

It was a quarter of an inch thick, five inches wide, and three and a half inches tall.

"At the factory, didn't Ms. Abbott say that they put a couple pieces of quarter-inch padding in each box to make sure there is no breakage?" asked Sara.

"Yes," said Jared.

"And maybe this is the quarter-inch padding that gets put in the box," continued Sara.

"Yes, maybe," agreed Daniel and Jared.

"And just suppose," Sara went on excitedly, "that a person left out the packing material. If you leave out a quarter of an inch on one side and a quarter of an inch on the other side, that adds up to half an inch! Then maybe you can fit some extra bottles in the box!"

"Wow!" said Daniel, "that could be how the thief is sneaking perfume out of the factory!"

"Hmmm," Jared mused, "and then they'd have a bunch of extra packing material to get rid of. They could just take that out the front door and pitch it in a dumpster."

"That's brilliant," Daniel said, "instead of trying to get the bottles out the front door, past the X-ray machine, they just ship extra bottles out in the shipping boxes!"

"But would that really work?" Jared asked.

"It all depends," said Sara thoughtfully, "on how big the shipping box is, compared to how big each individual Coralene box is."

They all considered that. How were they going to figure it out?

"I have that round Coralene box," said Sara

eventually, picking it up, "Let's measure it."

The little white cylinder was an inch in diameter, and almost three and a half inches tall.

"When we were in the factory, your mom measured the shipping box," Daniel pointed out, "so maybe you can sneak a peek at her notes?"

Jared and Sara looked at each other. "Her tablet is password protected," protested Jared. In any case, they didn't like the thought of meddling with one of their mom's computers.

"Maybe we can just ask her what the measurement was," Jared suggested.

"Fine, *you* ask," said Daniel.

During lunch, Jared thought about whether it was better to ask in a roundabout way, or just come straight out and ask. Finally, he decided asking straight out was better.

After lunch, his mother barely looked up from her tablet when Jared asked her about the box size. "Five inches by four and a half," she answered, "and just over three and a half inches tall." She said it distractedly as if her mind was still with whatever work problem she was struggling with.

Sara wanted to figure out how the little round boxes were arranged in the shipping boxes right away, but Jared and their father were putting on jackets and getting ready to leave.

"Guitar lesson," said Jared.

"Come on, Daniel, it's raining. I'll drop you at home," said Mr. Felton.

Sara found herself alone with a list of measurements. She got some black construction paper to represent the bottom of the box. Sara cut out a rectangle, five inches by four and a half. She found some lavender-colored paper and carefully traced around the base of the Coralene box with a pencil, making a circle with a diameter of one inch. Sara traced lots of circles and cut them out of the lavender paper. Then she got some light-green paper to represent the padding. The paper was not the same lime green as the foam, but that didn't matter. Sara just wanted to figure out how many bottles could go in the box. Sara cut two quarter-inch strips from the green paper.

What was it that Ms. Abbott had said? 'The box holds twenty bottles in four rows, each with five bottles.'

Well, that should be easy enough to check.

Sara put four rows with five circles each on top of the black rectangle. She placed her two strips of green paper on the edges.

The whole thing looked like this:

Everything fit perfectly. *What happens if I take out the green padding?* Sara wondered, *Can I fit more bottles in?* She took off the green paper strips.

Then she shifted all the purple circles down a bit. She tried to add another row, but it just wouldn't fit. The extra row of circles stuck out past the edge of the box.

Now it looked like this:

So, you couldn't just fit a fifth row of bottles in there. Sara was disappointed. She decided to wait for Jared and Daniel to discuss it.

But after Jared's guitar lesson, Sara had to return some books at the library, and then the Jones family was going out to a Junior Theatre performance, and so the rest of Saturday passed without a chance for Sara to show Jared and Daniel what she had done.

On Sunday morning, Daniel and Jared and Sara had just reconvened in the Felton house when Sara saw a text on her phone from Kevin.

"Can I come talk 2 u?" it said.

She showed the text to Daniel and Jared and they both nodded, so she wrote back, "Sure, any time."

Kevin rang the doorbell three minutes later. He must have been right around the corner when he texted. "Sundays at my house are boring," he explained. "What are you guys doing?"

Daniel explained about the visit to Mistral, and their thoughts concerning the theft. Sara showed them all her paper pieces, and how an extra row of bottles would not fit in the box.

"Drat!" Daniel griped, "I thought we had solved everything when we figured out about the shipping boxes."

"Well," Jared asked, "if they can't take product out the front door because of the X-ray machine,

131

and they're not sneaking out extra bottles in the shipping boxes, how is the thief getting it out?"

"What about the windows?" suggested Sara. "Couldn't you wrap up a bottle in some padding, and drop it out of the window, and then go collect it later, after you've walked out the front door?"

"I thought of that," said Kevin, "but my mom said the windows don't open."

"What about other exits from the building, other than the front door?" offered Daniel.

"Hmm, that's a good idea," said Sara. "You could open some side door, put a bag of Coralene outside, and then collect it later."

"There are a bunch of exits," said Kevin, "there have to be, in case there's a fire, but they all have alarms. You can't open any of the emergency exits without setting off an alarm."

There was a long silence at this point. Sara was staring at the little purple circles on the black paper. *There must be a way to make them fit.*

After some thought, Daniel said "What about the garbage? Couldn't someone put some Coralene in a garbage bin? When the janitor takes it out, they don't X-ray all the garbage leaving the building, do they?"

Kevin blinked. "I don't know," he mumbled, "I don't know what happens with the garbage."

Daniel looked at Sara, to see what she thought of his idea. But Sara was still staring at the circles.

"Hexagons," Sara whispered.

"Excuse me?" said Kevin.

"Hexagons," Sara repeated, "Hexagonal packing. That's it." She started to re-arrange the circles.

First, she removed one circle from the second row:

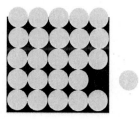

Then she shifted that row of circles sideways and down a bit. She also shifted the third row down:

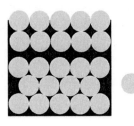

Next, Sara removed a circle from the fourth row, and then shifted the remaining circles in that row sideways and down a bit:

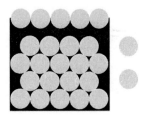

Finally she shifted the fifth row down:

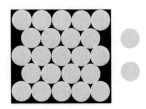

Now there was room for the fifth row! And there were 23 bottles in the box, not 20!

"You can't fit a whole row of five in, but you can fit an extra three bottles!" exclaimed Daniel.

"What did you call it – hexagonal something?" asked Kevin.

"Hexagonal packing," answered Sara, "that's what my mom called it."

They all looked at the little pieces of paper for a while. There was a long silence.

"Which people at Mistral would be able to do this?" asked Daniel.

"You'd have to have an accomplice on the outside," said Jared, "the person who receives the shipping box with the extra bottles. You'd have to know which boxes were going where."

Everyone looked at Kevin.

"Well," he said slowly, "there's Mr. Warren, who's in charge of shipping, and there's Ms. Abbott, the Facilities Manager. My mom says she has access to everything too. She's married to the owner's son. And there's Penelope Lee, the General Manager. She's the owner's daughter."

"Anyone else?" asked Jared.

Nobody wanted to say the obvious– that Kevin's mother was manager of operations, so she probably had access to everything too.

"It's not my mom," said Kevin fiercely.

"No, it's not your mom," agreed Sara, "but it's not Penelope Lee, either. She's my mom's friend."

"So it's either Mr. Warren or Ms. Abbott," Jared concluded, "but how can we prove anything? We've got no proof."

There was another long silence.

"Whoever is doing this is dumping the extra packing material in the dumpster," said Sara finally, "so maybe we could just watch the dumpster."

"Bad idea," said Daniel, "The person might go for weeks without dumping anything. And they could use a different dumpster. And we have to go to school; we can't sit there watching the dumpster."

In the end, they could not think of any way to catch the thief, so they agreed to think about it some more.

After Kevin and Daniel left, and Jared went off to do homework, Sara stayed and stared at the papers on her table for a long time. She pulled out her phone and took a picture of the arrangement of papers on the table. Then she swept all the little bits of paper into the trash bin.

She was sure they were on the right track. But how to prove it?

9
MAKING A PLAN

During lunch at school on Monday, Jared asked "What if we confront both of them?".

He was so interested in the problem that he was sitting with his sister and Daniel and Kevin instead of the group of friends he usually sat with. "You know, Ms. Abbott and Mr. Warren.

I don't mean directly confront them, but maybe put a note on their doorsteps? The note could say 'we know you're the thief!' We could hide somewhere nearby and wait until they come out. Then we could watch how they react when they read it."

"That's not very convincing," said Kevin skeptically, "Would they be scared by a note that says 'we know you're the thief'?"

"Well, we could maybe take a photo of the dumpster," suggested Sara, "and take one of those green padding sheets and put it with the note, and then the person would know that someone knows exactly what they're up to."

"It's a good idea," agreed Daniel, "but maybe we should just do Mr. Warren."

Daniel had not forgotten how Mr. Warren had treated him at the factory.

"My mom actually likes Mr. Warren," said Kevin. "I think we should do it to Ms. Abbott."

In the end, they agreed that Sara and Daniel would leave the note and the materials at Mr. Warren's house, and Jared and Kevin would do the same at Ms. Abbott's house.

It wasn't going to happen right away. There were many things that needed to be done first. In fact, there were four jobs, which divided up perfectly among the four of them.

First someone had to talk to Nayla to find out where that dumpster was and then go there and take a photo. Kevin volunteered.

Someone would have to find the addresses of Ms. Abbott and Mr. Warren and scout the locations online. Jared offered to take on this task because it mostly involved being on the computer, which suited him just fine. He would need to check online for the street view, to see whether there was a tree or a hedge, or something else, nearby to hide behind. He would also check the bus routes, to see how to get to each of the houses.

Someone would have to access the Mosaic Club material store and swipe another piece of that green foam. They had the piece Sara snuck out of the factory, but they needed a second one. Daniel agreed to be in charge of that. He started referring to himself as the Green Foam Swiper and sketched out an Anime drawing of a superhero of that name.

And lastly someone was going to have to print out the notes. Sara said she'd take care of that. It wasn't like composing a poem – all she had to write was "We know you did it!" and then print two copies.

Kevin said he would email the dumpster photo to Sara. She also had a sudden inspiration to print out some fake survey questions. They could carry those on a clipboard with a pen in case someone opened the door as they walked up to it. They could then pretend they were there to ask a few survey questions.

It seemed as though they had all the tasks and possibilities worked out.

"Excellent behavior at the table," Jared whispered to Sara right before dinner time, "And act natural — we don't want Mom or Dad to suspect anything."

"How was school?" asked Mr. Felton, as they sat down to dinner.

"Wonderful," said Sara.

"Just great," said Jared, followed by "Would you please pass the salad?" and "Thank you."

Mr. and Mrs. Felton exchanged glances.

It occurred to Sara that perhaps *excellent behavior* and *acting natural* were slightly contradictory events. She tried to think of something to say that didn't have anything to do with their plan. She couldn't, so she stayed silent.

Fortunately, the doorbell rang, and Sara jumped up to get it. It was Uncle Charles, with Isabelle.

"Hello Aunt Sam! Hello Uncle Dennis!" said

142

Isabelle cheerfully, looking around to see if there was any dessert.

Sara's phone chirped and she checked it. It was a text from Kevin. "Dumpster photo for u" it said. Her heart pounded. They were really going to do this!

"Why hello, Isabelle," said Mr. Felton, ruffling her hair, "What brings you here?"

Mr. Jones said, "I had an interesting phone call today from Isabelle's teacher."

He looked meaningfully at his sister.

"Oh yes?" Mrs. Felton asked, eating a spoonful of peach cobbler, "What about?"

"She asked for a substantial donation so the school can buy more toys for Isabelle's classroom," he said.

"*Seriously?*" Mr. Felton was startled, "a charitable donation to buy *more toys?*"

"Apparently," Mr. Jones said pleasantly, "my dear sister, Samantha, told Isabelle that her preschool

143

doesn't have enough toys, and Isabelle repeated that to Ms. McGann."

"What!" exclaimed Mrs. Felton in surprise, "I never said that! When Sara and Jared were there, that preschool had *tons* of toys, *boxes and boxes* of toys. That's ridiculous."

Everyone looked at Isabelle, who was calmly spooning a large helping of peach cobbler onto a plate.

Isabelle looked up. "But you *did* say it, Aunt Sam. When we were talking about optization, and picking up toys. When *I said* that I only picked up five. And *you said* that there weren't enough toys." Isabelle smiled sweetly.

Mrs. Felton looked appalled.

"She's right, Mom," chortled Jared, "You did say it."

"I just meant," Mrs. Felton sputtered, "that to win the toy-pick-up race with Alicia, Isabelle had to move fast, because if she went slowly the other kids would get them first... there weren't enough toys to just win by keeping on picking up more and more...." Mrs. Felton's voice trailed off.

She looked at Isabelle. Isabelle was now eating the peach cobbler and savoring her triumph.

"She's got a splendid knack for taking things out of context and twisting them to her advantage, hasn't she?" said Mr. Felton.

"Takes after her mother," Mr. Jones said, looking fondly at his daughter.

"But even though Alicia won that race," said Isabelle, "I won the coin toss for being stalker."

"What on earth are you talking about?" asked Mr. Felton.

Sara decided this would be an opportune moment to leave the table.

Isabelle started to explain something about a haunted house, and how she and Alicia had both wanted the stalker part, because if you were the stalker you could jump out and grab people.

145

Sara sent her pages to the computer printer. The first page said, "WE KNOW YOU DID IT!" Sara printed two copies. The second item was the dumpster photo from Kevin. And there was an environmental survey, which had questions such as "Have you considered putting solar energy panels on your house?" Sara sent those pages to the printer too.

Isabelle was still providing the perfect distraction. The grown-ups were horrified but enthralled by her account of how Alicia was stuck with the boring job of being a head-on-a-plate while Isabelle got to stalk people.

Isabelle added that if *she* had to be the head on the plate in the haunted house, she would be the kind of head that *leaps* off the plate.

Sara collected her pages from the printer.

She put them in a folder on her desk, so no grown-up would happen to see them and ask inconvenient questions. It would be hard to explain why she had printed out two photos of a dumpster.

Over in the kitchen, Sara could just hear Isabelle's story ending with an account of how Alicia accused Isabelle of squashing the witch's pointy hat, which Isabelle denied. Fortunately, the teacher believed her, or she would have lost her stalker job. Mr. and Mrs. Felton reacted with suitable dismay at the near disaster.

Sara took another long look at the dumpster photos and accusation statements that she had printed out. There were two sets, but presumably only one person was guilty, so they'd be accusing an innocent person too. Sara closed the folder and set it down, but she couldn't shake her uneasy feeling.

10 Accusations

All of Tuesday – school, lunch clubs, and dinner – passed in a blur. As planned, Jared and Sara told their parents they were going to Daniel's house, and Daniel told his parents he was going to Sara's house. Kevin had eaten at Daniel's, so his mother thought he was still there.

The four met at the bus stop, and Sara waved the important folder at them. Jared remembered the clipboards and ran back home to sneak them out of the garage. He got back just as the bus was pulling up to the stop.

After two stops, Kevin and Jared got off the bus. Daniel and Sara had farther to go.

Kevin and Jared turned left off the main street and walked towards Ms. Abbott's house. This visit was going to be the easier of the two, Jared explained, because the online street view had shown a nice hedge out front. Jared held the pen and the clipboard containing the made-up environmental survey. Kevin held the folder with the dumpster photo, the note, and the green foam rectangle.

It suddenly occurred to Jared that they didn't both need to approach the door. If you wanted to put something in front of the door, ring the doorbell, and then run away as fast as you could, it wouldn't help to have a second person running as well.

"Let me have the folder," he said to Kevin, "we don't need both of us up there."

Kevin handed over the folder. When they were in front of the house, Kevin crouched behind the hedge. He found a thin part, through which he could just about see the door of the house. Kevin decided it would be best to pull out his phone, and pretend to be looking at it, in case anyone wondered why he was lingering there on the sidewalk.

Jared walked up the front pathway to the house. He was not particularly nervous. Partly it was because Ms. Abbott was just not a scary person, but also because he had the clipboard in his hand. If anything happened right now, before he got to the door – if anyone came out now and saw him, he could just say he was there to do an environmental survey.

There was still a way out. But his heart was beating loudly in anticipation.

The house was quiet, but there was a light on upstairs. Was someone home?

Jared slowed his steps. It was almost as though he was hoping someone would open the door – Ms. Abbott's husband perhaps – and Jared could just say "Have you considered solar energy panels?" But the door was still firmly shut when he reached it, so he bent down and set the folder on the welcome mat. He took a deep breath, jabbed the doorbell with his finger, sprinted down the five steps and down the flagstone path, and then ducked behind the hedge, panting for breath. Kevin looked at him in wide-eyed admiration and then pointed silently.

Someone had opened the door of the house.

It was a young woman – not Ms. Abbott. The woman wore sweatpants and a T-shirt. She looked like a college student. The woman glanced around curiously and was about to shut the door when she noticed the folder on the ground. Picking it up, she stepped back inside and closed the door. Kevin and Jared could hear the click of the lock. Then there was silence again.

The boys looked at each other in disappointment. That had not been useful *at all.* Jared made a face and pulled out his phone to send a text to Sara and Daniel. Then they crept away from the hedge. Once they were safely down the street, they walked back to the bus stop, trying to act as normal as possible.

Sara and Daniel had a longer walk to get to Mr. Warren's house from the bus stop. They were still walking to the house when they got Jared's text.

"Oh, that's too bad," said Sara, "Maybe that woman was Ms. Abbott's babysitter or housekeeper or something."

"Should we call this off?" Daniel asked, remembering how mean Mr. Warren was to them.

He didn't relish the idea of getting caught.

"No," Sara said confidently. "Let's do it. I didn't think Ms. Abbott was the thief anyway, so if she gets some random note and a picture of a dumpster from her babysitter, she won't have any idea what it's about, so no harm done."

As they approached Mr. Warren's house, Daniel dragged his feet. He admitted to himself that Mr. Warren scared him.

There was, unfortunately, no hedge in front of this house. Sara and Daniel walked right past the house and kept on going, to scout the scene. There were a couple of trees, but they were too small to hide behind.

"Plan B," Sara said in a low voice, even though there was no one else out on the street at this time of evening. Daniel nodded toward a blue minivan parked on the street. They could duck behind that, but it was not ideal. Anyone could see them from across the street, but the house there was dark.

With luck, the residents wouldn't be returning for a while. At least it was a quiet, wide street and the houses were well separated.

Jared's text had suggested that only one person should approach the door, rather than two. At the end of the block, they flipped a coin to see who would do it. Sara lost. As they walked back down the street, Sara felt her heart beating faster.

I'm just here to do an environmental survey, she reminded herself.

Daniel crouched down behind the blue minivan as Sara approached the front porch.

"Have you considered solar energy panels?" Sara whispered to herself.

No dawdling. She put the folder on the ground, rang the doorbell, and ran.

She desperately wanted to turn around and see if anyone was at the door, but she didn't dare until she was safely behind the minivan, gasping for breath.

A moment later, the door opened. It was Mr. Warren! "Who is it?" he called in his harsh way, picking up the folder, and looking up and down the street.

"Come here, boy," he called, and Daniel and Sara were horrified to see a dog appear in the doorway next to him.

"Run!" Sara whispered urgently to Daniel, and then she bolted down the street. But Daniel was frozen with fear. It was a big dog, with big teeth. He had dreams about dogs like this. Bad dreams.

Mr. Warren came down the stairs of his front porch, holding his dog by the collar with one hand and the folder in the other.

"Hey, you!" he called out, looking down the street after Sara.

Daniel was still crouched motionless behind the parked car. *Why did Sara run? Now he's seen her!*

Sara looked back. Daniel was still crouched behind the car. Mr. Warren was advancing slowly towards the street, but he was looking in her direction. It was twilight – would Mr. Warren recognize her at this distance, and in this low light? And why wasn't Daniel running? Then she remembered her cousin's fear of big dogs, and she groaned.

And then, as if things couldn't get any worse, a car appeared at the far end of the street, driving slowly towards them. And it wasn't just any car; it was a police car! The headlights illuminated Daniel like a spotlight.

Sara stopped abruptly. Running was not the right thing in this situation. She slowly turned around. Her heart was racing. She forced herself to walk back toward Daniel and the police car.

Daniel stood up and moved towards the sidewalk.

"You!" yelled Mr. Warren, "the kid with the RFID lady! What are you doing here?"

The police car pulled over.

"What's happening here?" said the police officer, confronting Daniel, Mr. Warren, and the dog.

But this wasn't just any police officer. This was someone they knew.

With a shaky voice, Daniel said "Uh, hello Detective! It's Daniel Jones, do you remember me?"

Sara came up next to them, out of breath, panting.

"Oh, Daniel," said Detective Carson, "and Sara! Of course, I remember you, from the bank!"

Well, if there was one advantage in being held up in a bank robbery, it was that the police would remember you kindly later.

"These kids were playing some sort of prank on me!" complained Mr. Warren, waving the folder in the dim light. "Ringing my doorbell, then running away!" He opened the folder. "What is this nonsense? What is this? A dumpster?"

He showed Detective Carson the picture of the dumpster.

By this point, Sara had recovered her wits.

"Dumpster?" she said, pretending to be surprised. "Oh, that's a mistake, I put the wrong folder on your step. I meant to leave you this survey."

Sara took the survey page from her clipboard and handed it to Mr. Warren.

"We're doing a survey about environmental issues," Daniel chimed in, "Have you considered getting solar energy panels?"

"What? Here? With this cloudy weather?" Mr. Warren still sounded angry, but not as much as before. He turned his back on them.

"Come on, boy," he said, and Daniel and Sara were relieved to see Mr. Warren and the dog retreat to the house.

Detective Carson was holding the folder now. He looked at the note, which said "WE KNOW

YOU DID IT" and at the picture of the dumpster, and at the piece of green foam. Then he looked at Sara and Daniel.

Their faces were carefully neutral.

Finally, he said, "Well – Sara, Daniel – would you like a ride home?"

"Oh, yes! Thank you!" they both said at once. Sara quietly texted Jared not to wait for them at the bus stop and told him she would explain later.

On the drive home, Sara and Daniel did their best to set aside all thoughts of Mr. Warren and the disappointing results of the evening. They just prattled on to Detective Carson about the Mosaic Club, and the Anime Club, and the upcoming orange picking event.

When they were almost home, Daniel even asked the detective whether he had considered getting solar electricity panels. Detective Carson said "No, Daniel, I haven't," but something in his tone said *Don't mess with me, son.* Daniel shut up fast.

At Sara's house, they both politely said, "Thanks very much for the ride". Detective Carson said, "Don't mention it". He watched them from his car until they were safely indoors before driving away.

11

ORANGE PICKING

The mood on Wednesday was glum. The four went disconsolately through all the details of the night before and concluded that their plan had not worked. Mr. Warren hadn't read the note in the folder, and he hadn't reacted to the photograph of the dumpster.

And they hadn't learned anything from Ms. Abbott either. Who knew whether the babysitter, if that's who it was, had even given the folder to Ms. Abbott? Perhaps the young woman had thrown it out – they'd forgotten to address the folder to Ms. Abbott.

To add to the general misery, Tom came to school bragging that he'd won the M&M counting contest at the Screamery.

Tom was very smug about it. He'd purchased a phone app called Candy Count 'Em which estimated how many candies were in a jar, if you just took a couple of photos of it. Of course, the app knew all about M&Ms, and some computer programmer must have programmed in how random packing fractions worked.

Daniel thought it was cheating to use a candy counter app, but he didn't say anything, possibly because his own estimation method hadn't been – strictly speaking – totally honest since he'd sort of, kind of, *almost* touched the container when he'd used the string to measure its circumference. But still he thought there was a big difference between making a calculation yourself and just having your phone do it all from a photo.

Kevin was the gloomiest of all of them. His mom had told him the night before that they might have to move again soon.

The others didn't know what to say to that, but Daniel offered him a granola bar from his lunch bag.

As usual Daniel was the first to bounce back. On Friday he was consulting with Sara and Kevin on the importance of arriving early for the fruit-picking event, which was scheduled for Sunday.

On Saturday evening Sara and Daniel and Jared were playing catch with an orange in the kitchen while they talked about the event. Sara wondered how Kevin was doing, and thought it was too bad that the teams were limited to three people.

"I'm not going to be able to drive you guys tomorrow," her mom said as she ended a phone call. "Penelope just called, and she needs to talk to me."

Sara dropped the orange.

She exchanged glances with Daniel and Jared.

"Did she say what it was about?" Jared asked casually.

"She said they're not going to do an RFID system." Mrs. Felton looked kind of worried. "I hope the company is doing okay."

Daniel, Jared and Sara said nothing. They were all wondering *why* Mistral would be discarding plans for the RFID system.

Did they not have enough money to install such a system?

Sara was also thinking about Kevin, and whether he and his mom were going to be okay.

"I'll check in with Charles and Claudine," said Mrs. Felton. "Maybe one of them can drive."

The next day dawned cool and clear – perfect weather for being active outdoors.

Daniel's mother drove. Daniel's father liked to tease that she drove as if she were a NASCAR driver in a video game. Indeed, it only took thirty minutes to get to the grove. When they arrived, Miss Robinson was already there, handing out water bottles.

Mrs. Jones handed a bottle of sunscreen to the teacher in case anyone forgot theirs, and they chatted a bit.

Miss Robinson called out to Sara, Daniel, and Jared: "Remember to look for insects! Take a photo if you see anything interesting. And call me over!"

Daniel looked over the grove. There were only two cumquat trees and one very small grapefruit tree – the rest were all orange trees.

"Are the cumquats and grapefruit for picking," asked Daniel, "or just the oranges?"

"Oh, yes," answered Miss Robinson, "everything gets picked."

Sara pulled Daniel and Jared aside to discuss strategy. "I think," she said, "that this is like the situation with Isabelle and the toys."

Jared and Daniel looked around.

"You mean," said Daniel, "that we're going to run out of fruit to pick, just the way Isabelle ran out of toys to pick up?"

"Precisely," said Sara.

Privately, Daniel thought she sounded just like her mother. "This grove is going to run out of fruit, and especially the two cumquat trees are going to run out. If we want small stuff to poke around the box edges, we'd better nab those first."

"Maybe you should do it," said Daniel to Sara. "Tom won't be focusing on you."

"And we all have to pick fast," said Jared.

"I brought some bags," said Sara, "so we can fill

166

those first and then repack the fruit neatly in HCP format in the boxes."

Tom arrived with Marisa and Kate. Miss Robinson handed everyone long poles. Little metal baskets were attached at the ends, with curved prongs. The fruit that was low down could be picked with your hands, but for an orange high up, you had to maneuver the orange into the little basket, under the curved prongs, and then yank it off.

"Take your time, people," said Miss Robinson, "Just be safe. We're not in a hurry." She did not know about Daniel's twenty-dollar wager with Tom, and he hoped to keep it that way. He was sure she would not approve.

Most of the class started picking with the poles because it looked like fun and because they were under no pressure. But Jared and Daniel focused on grabbing the low-hanging fruit, which were easy to pick.

It took twenty minutes for Sara to strip the two cumquat trees. She collected hundreds of the small fruit.

Halfway through, Tom sauntered over. "It's stupid, picking cumquats," he said. "They're too small."

He went back to the orange trees. In less than two hours, the horde of children picked the small grove clean.

Jared, Sara and Daniel worked on transferring their fruit from the bags to the boxes.

First they placed a hexagonal layer of oranges in the bottom of each box and filled all the gaps around the edge with cumquats.

Then they placed a second hexagonal layer of oranges on top of the first one, arranged so that each orange nestled tightly with the ones in the bottom row. More cumquats were used to fill in all the gaps around the edge of the layer of oranges. A third hexagonal layer of oranges, with cumquats around the edge, filled the box completely, with no gaps at all. They repeated this until they filled all six of their boxes. Each box represented an exquisite work of precise, dense, packing.

All the children assembled their boxes in one spot, where the truck was going to collect them for the food bank. Tom and Marisa and Kate looked pleased with themselves. Their six boxes were nearly full, in a haphazard sort of way.

Jared and Daniel and Sara brought their boxes over, one at a time, struggling with the weight.

Daniel said to Tom "Were you counting on more *pieces* of fruit, or more *weight* of fruit?"

"Uh, dunno," said Tom, who clearly hadn't thought about the details.

"Well, it doesn't really matter," said Daniel, "because we win either way."

Tom looked at the boxes. Each box was completely, utterly full. The oranges at the top were in a perfect hexagonal arrangement, flat and neatly nestled on top of the layer below. The space around the edges was stuffed with cumquats.

Tom's jaw tightened a bit as he looked at the six boxes, but he didn't say anything.

"Cumquats are pretty handy, actually," Sara couldn't resist saying to him. Tom didn't look at her. He just walked over to Daniel, fishing around in his jacket pockets. He handed him a twenty-dollar bill and muttered "Good job." Daniel could not stop grinning, but instead of taunting Tom about losing, he didn't say anything. Sara thought that was very mature of her cousin.

A little while later, Mrs. Jones picked them up.

"I have to get Isabelle from ballet," she said, "so you're all having lunch at Sara and Jared's house."

Just before they reached home, Sara's cell phone chirped with a text from Kevin. "Can I come over? Need to talk."

"Sure" she typed in, along with "Orange picking WIN!"

When they got home, Sara and Jared knew something was wrong. Their parents stood in the living room talking, but as soon as they saw the children they stopped.

There was an awkward moment of silence, and Sara knew that it must have been an important conversation.

But her mom just asked, "How was the orange picking?"

"We won!" said Daniel, displaying the twenty-dollar bill. "Thanks to hexagonal packing!"

"And how was your meeting with Ms. Lee?" asked Sara, "Why don't they want the RFID system any more?"

"Funny you should ask." Her mother gave her a long look. "It seems that, rather remarkably, the problems at the factory are going to quietly resolve themselves."

"What!" yelped Sara, at the same instant that Daniel said, "The thief was caught?"

"No, the thief was not caught. And *nobody* has admitted to *anything*. But Ms. Abbott has apparently decided to resign her position. She won't be working at Mistral any longer," Mrs. Felton said, in a quiet, thoughtful way.

The children looked at each other in surprise.

"I think she's going to be getting help for some problems." Mrs. Felton sighed. "I don't even know what her problems are. Maybe a gambling addiction. But anyway, she's resigning, and the family is being quiet about it because she's Oscar's wife, and there's nothing public, but that's the end of the matter."

"Wow," said Jared, "that's amazing, I guess now things can go back to normal at Mistral."

"Yes," said Mrs. Felton.

There was a silence. It was almost as though Mrs. Felton was waiting for them to say something.

Finally, Mrs. Felton added "Penelope said that Ms. Abbott decided to resign because of a note that someone put on her doorstep. A strange note with a strange photograph."

Sara felt her parents looking at her in particular.

"You know," said her father, "there was one strikingly odd thing about the note and the photo. It's what was written *on the back*."

Sara froze. *You mean that hadn't been fresh paper in the printer?* she thought to herself, but she didn't say anything.

Jared and Daniel looked at her in alarm. Finally, Sara squeaked "Something on the back?"

"Yes," her mother went on smoothly. "There was the name Helga Gisladottir on the back of one paper, and a similar foreign name on the other piece of paper. Penelope at first had no idea what kind of name that was."

Sara swallowed, struggling to regain her composure. *Oh no! My pen pal!*

"Say," her father said neutrally, "Sara, doesn't that sound like one of your Icelandic pen pals?"

173

"It's a very common Icelandic name," Jared managed to say, coming to Sara's rescue.

"Yes," agreed Mrs. Felton, soothingly, "it occurred to Penelope that maybe it was an Icelandic name. I don't know what gave her that idea. Maybe it was that she remembered me talking about Icelandic pen pals."

Sara finally was able to look up. It was clear that her mom was not angry.

"In the end, Penelope was relieved that the theft has been solved, and nobody is going to get fired, and they don't need the RFID system," Mrs. Felton said.

"But shouldn't Ms. Abbott get punished, if she's the thief?" protested Sara.

"Yeah," added Daniel, "and her accomplice on the outside..."

"You mean," interrupted Jared, *just supposing* she had an accomplice on the outside."

"That's what I meant," Daniel corrected himself,

"*supposing* there was an accomplice on the outside, shouldn't that person get punished too?"

"Sometimes justice does not get properly served," Mr. Felton acknowledged ruefully. "Sometimes you just have to be satisfied that a bad action stops."

Mrs. Felton pulled an envelope out of her pocket. It had some cash in it. She emptied it onto the table.

"Penelope gave me this as a present for you kids, thirty dollars for each of you. I can't imagine why. Maybe she felt bad that she was not going to be hiring me to do an RFID system after all."

Mrs. Felton yawned and stretched. Mr. Felton checked his phone.

"Oh, by the way," he added casually, "I got a phone call from Detective Carson. Awfully nice of him to give you a ride home the other day from Mr. Warren's house. I hope you thanked him."

How much do they actually know? thought Sara, Jared and Daniel.

Clearly, the grown-ups knew rather more than they had said.

After his aunt and uncle went into the kitchen to start making lunch, Daniel immediately pocketed his thirty dollars. It went very nicely in his pocket, next to the twenty dollars he had won in the wager. *Now I have enough to buy Submarine Traitors!* thought Daniel.

"What about Kevin?" Sara asked. "Shouldn't he get some of this money?"

"Good point," said Jared promptly.

But Daniel looked a bit unhappy. He put his hand very slowly into his pocket and felt the wad of bills.

"Look, you can keep my share of Tom's twenty dollars," offered Sara.

Daniel's expression became even more grim – he hadn't realized that Sara was expecting a share of the orange-picking wager.

The doorbell rang, and Kevin bounced in.

"Guess what? My mom is not getting fired! In fact, she's getting a raise!"

"That's great!" Sara enthused.

"Yeah! Hector Lee told her this morning. Ms. Abbott is resigning her job! I think that means Ms. Abbott was the thief, don't you? And my mom is not under suspicion any more. Do you think our note had something to do with it?"

"We know it did," Sara answered. "Penelope just talked to my mom."

"I have something else I have to tell you," Kevin said. and suddenly he didn't look so happy. "I was the one who spray-painted the wall." Kevin looked around at their faces to gauge their reaction.

He fiddled for a moment with the zipper on his jacket pocket, and then spoke in a rush. "I'm sorry I did it, and I'm sorry I lied to you. I was just really mad, and I wanted the newspaper people to see it. I don't know what I was thinking."

Sara was shocked. She had convinced herself

that Kevin wasn't lying when he said he didn't do it. Sara didn't approve of vandalism, or of lying to a friend.

Jared, however, was not shocked. When he'd heard about Kevin putting the spray cans in Daniel's backpack, Jared had figured that Kevin had done the spraying, too.

"Well, it's over now," Jared said. "And Penelope gave my mom a present for all of us," Jared gestured at the remaining money on the table. "I suppose it's for saying thanks for helping to catch the thief. You should get a share."

"No, you guys keep it," said Kevin, "My mom gets to keep her job, which means we get to stay here. That's enough for me. Look, I've got to go, my mom's waiting. I just wanted to let you know."

After Kevin left, Daniel took his hand out of his pocket. The fifty dollars was safe in there. He had enough to buy the video game, but there was also a skateboard he had his eye on.

Daniel started thinking *What kind of bet can I make with my cousins? or with Tom?* After all, Submarine Traitors wasn't coming out for another month, and Tom still had thirty dollars from guessing the number of M&Ms at the Screamery. There was no reason why Daniel shouldn't plan on making that money his own.

Sara was not thinking about the money; she was thinking about Kevin, and about Ms. Abbott. Because Ms. Abbott would no longer be working at Mistral, the thefts would stop.

It was good that Ms. Reynolds would not lose her job. Kevin would not have to move to another city again. Perhaps no one at Mistral outside of the Lee family would know that Ms. Abbott was guilty. And nobody at Mistral would know the whole story.

Maybe it was better this way.

Life would be really terrible for Ms. Abbott's two children if their mom had to go to jail.

On the other hand, Sara thought that people should be punished for doing wrong. On the *other* other hand, Ms. Abbott had lost her job, so that was a kind of punishment.

Kevin wasn't getting punished for his vandalism either. Sara would have to persuade him to confess to the principal. It was the right thing to do. Maybe if Kevin came forward and confessed, now that it was two weeks later, and he was no longer in any danger of getting caught, Principal Stevens would go easy on him. Perhaps he would just have to do some community service, like picking up trash in the playground.

That night, while getting ready for bed, Sara held the little Coralene box. The lavender flowers were printed in a way that seemed almost like engraving.

Thoughtfully, Sara traced the circling spray around the Coralene cylinder with her finger.

Packing cylinders or oranges in boxes in neat

hexagonal rows was so much more orderly than the messiness of real life.

If you could tessellate mosaic tiles in a two-dimensional plane and oranges in a three-dimensional box, maybe you could tessellate in higher dimensions too?

How about eight-dimensional space – what would such tiles even look like?

Sara tried to picture tiles in eight dimensions, shapes that twisted and stretched across space and time and distant stars and consciousness.

She would have to talk to Mrs. Rao tomorrow and ask her whether there was an eight-dimensional space, and what tiles looked like in it.

Her mom stuck her head in the door and said "Guess what? In two weeks, Uncle George is coming for a long weekend."

Sara looked up with delight.

Interesting things usually happened when Uncle George came to visit.

Sara wished her mom good night and lay back in bed, her mind wandering.

I wonder if Ms. Lee would let us learn more about that awesome chemistry lab? Can I get Mom to buy me a better calculator? I wonder what Detective Carson is investigating now. And next time I have to be more careful with the printer paper.

THESE IDEAS IN THE REAL WORLD

Here are some notes about the ideas you read about in the story.

TESSELLATION:

A *tile* is often a thin rectangular piece of baked clay or cut stone. Tiles are often used to cover a floor in a house, or a wall, or a roof. We can use the word *tile* as a verb to mean *to cover something with tiles*. There is also a fancy verb *to tessellate* which means the same thing.

When we think about tessellating a two-dimensional surface, such as a piece of paper or a wall, we usually think about regular polygons.

As Sara said in the story, a regular polygon is a shape in which all the sides have the same length, and they have the same angle from one to another.

Here are some regular polygons. What are the names of these five shapes?

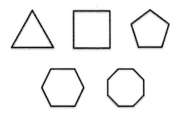

(The answer is at the end.)

There are only three regular polygons that can be used to tile the plane with no gaps between them: triangles, squares and hexagons. There are many kinds of triangles, rectangles and hexagons – not just regular ones – that can tessellate a two-dimensional surface without any gaps:

TESSELLATION IN ART:

Sometimes tiles are used to make pretty designs, called *mosaics*. The word "tessera" is a special word that means "tile," especially when you are talking about a tile that is used in a mosaic. Because the word tessera comes from Latin (and before that from Greek), the plural of tessera is *not* tesseras. Instead, the plural is *tesserae*.

There are many mosaic floors and walls from ancient Rome and Greece, and from other ancient civilizations. Sometimes the artists used regular polygons but often they used irregular shapes.

185

If you want to make a repeating pattern, you can use shapes other than regular polygons.

Here is a tessellation made of arrows:

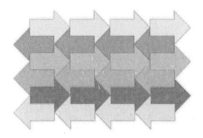

If we wanted to, we could cover a big paper or a wall using just this arrow shape, and there would be no gaps. But notice that the arrow sometimes points forwards, and sometimes points backwards. If we tried to do this with the shapes pointing the same direction, there would be gaps.

There is a whole area of art called *tessellation art*. People make very interesting shapes, such as birds or fish that fit perfectly into each other, with no gaps.

One of the most famous creators of tessellation art was the Dutch graphic artist, M. C. Escher. It's worth looking up his tessellations involving reptiles, birds and fish!

You might wonder which irregular shapes can tile a sheet of paper without any gaps.

Here is a polygon which is not regular:

Could we tile the plane with this?

Yes, we can!

We can put the shapes next to each other and they will perfectly fill up the whole space with no gaps:

What about this shape? Can we tile the plane with this one, with no gaps?

No, we can't. That does not work.

If you try to put two of them right next to each other, there will be little gaps:

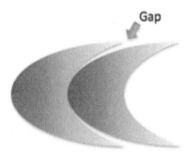

So how can we make an interesting shape which will work for tessellation?

Here's one way to do it. Start with one of the usual polygons which we know will work.

For example, we can start with a rectangle that we cut out of construction paper:

Then, cut out an interesting shape *from just one side* of the rectangle.

Here, we've cut out a lightning bolt, and a curvy shape:

Now, take the little pieces that you just cut out, and move them around to the opposite side, right above the place where you cut them out.

Attach them up there:

Now you've made a new, complicated, shape that will work perfectly for tessellating the whole space!

You can put lots of them next to each other and *they will fit with no gaps!*

You know it will work because the shapes that stick out the top will perfectly fit into the bottom of the tile above, since that is where they were cut from.

Here are a bunch of them together:

QUESTION:

Instead of cutting the bottom side (and moving the little pieces around to the top) can we cut the *right side* and move the little pieces around to the left?

Can we cut *both* the bottom side and the right side, and move the little pieces around to the top and the left? Will it still work?

If you're not sure, get out some paper and scissors and give it a try!

191

TESSELLATION IN MANUFACTURING:

Sometimes when people manufacture a car, or an airplane, or *something big* out of metal, they cut the parts out of big sheets.

There might be many pieces that have to be cut out of one metal sheet. It is like cutting a piece of paper, except harder and more expensive. The person doing the cutting has to plan *where to cut* in order to minimize waste.

The best way is often a tessellation.

When you cut things out of paper, you can think about tessellations too. Suppose, for a school project, you have to make a forest.

You will be cutting trees out of paper.

Here is one tree:

Suppose you need eight trees. You could cut them out of paper in a haphazard way – one over here, and one over there, like this:

But that would waste a lot of paper. Instead, you could try to tessellate the shape. It may not be possible to tessellate it exactly, with no gaps. But, this kind of shape is bigger at one end and smaller at the other. If you put one upright and the next one upside down, and follow that pattern, you don't waste much space – or much paper:

Now, we are thinking of the tree shapes as if they were tiles in a tessellation!

TREE SHAPE OPTIMIZATION:

So far, we've been thinking of creating a bunch of paper trees using the following approach:

Step 1: Draw a nice tree shape.
Step 2: Try to fit eight copies of that tree shape as close together as possible on the paper, to minimize waste.

Let's think of this problem of cutting eight trees from paper in terms of *optimization*, where we have an *objective function* – the thing we're trying to make as large (or as small) as possible, and some *constraints* – the limits on the situation.

How would we describe this process in terms of an optimization?

Well, for **Step 1**, the aim is to make a nice tree shape, but by itself this step is not really an optimization. The instructions do not say to make the tree as nice as possible, and even if they did say that, it would not be a well-defined objective function. Everyone might have a different idea of what *nice* is.

Looking at **Step 2**, we can recognize an objective function. The objective function is the amount of useful paper left over after we cut out eight trees, and we are trying to *make it as large as possible*. That is, we want to *maximize* it. One could just as well say that the objective function is the amount of paper getting wasted, and we are trying to *minimize* it or make it *as small as possible*.

For example, in the picture below, imagine that the two blue rectangles represent sheets of paper that we will use for cutting trees. The blue rectangles are the same size. For the sheet on the left, the eight trees are cut out any which way, and so the usable paper remaining is shown by the yellow dashed area. For the sheet of paper on the right, the trees are packed closer together, so the area of paper remaining after cutting out eight trees is larger.

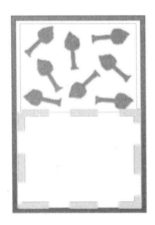 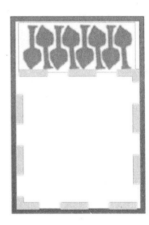

Remember that the objective function is the area of useful paper remaining after the trees are cut out, which is the yellow area. The tree-cutting on the right wastes less paper, so it gives us a larger value of the objective function.

We can think of Step 1 as specifying a constraint: the tree has to be nice (presumably that means it is at least recognizable as being a tree).

The challenge doesn't mention other constraints, but there probably are some. For example, we only have certain equipment available to use for this process (scissors, pencil, ruler).

Now, we could approach this problem in a different way. We could give ourselves the following problem:

Draw a nice recognizable tree shape subject to the constraint that it *tessellates the paper perfectly with no gaps*. This way, there would be no waste.

What would this look like? Well, here is an example of one tree shape that would work:

Here is how we would cut out eight copies of the tree shape without leaving any gaps:

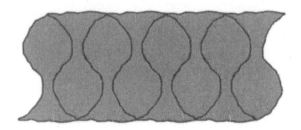

And there's an unexpected benefit from doing it this way: we also do *less cutting*. When you make *one cut* along the side of a tree, that cut is the edge of the tree to the left and also of the tree to the right.

So, this way we waste less paper and we also save time by doing less cutting!

QUESTION:

What is the disadvantage of doing it this way?

(The answer is at the end.)

TESSELLATION IN THREE DIMENSIONS:

So far, we've been talking about shapes filling up a flat surface, like a piece of paper, with no gaps. But there are lots of interesting situations where the same questions arise for three-dimensional space.

What kinds of shapes can fill up a space with no gaps? And how close together can you pack things like balls, so that you waste as little space as possible?

One of the first people to study this carefully was Thomas Harriot in 1587.

He was sailing across the Atlantic Ocean with Sir Walter Raleigh, who had lots of questions about the cannonballs on his ships.

What is the best way to pile them up?

How can I calculate how many cannonballs are in that pile?

Harriot found that face-centered cubic (FCC) packing and hexagonal close packing (HCP) are the best ways to pack round objects.

Fruit sellers around the world know this too. FCC and HCP stacking of oranges can be found in many fruit stalls and supermarkets.

Here, the goal is not only to fit as many oranges as possible into the space; the greengrocers are also concerned about stability and beauty.

You don't want the stack of oranges to fall down, and you want the fruit pile to look pretty.

Of course, Sir Walter was concerned about stability and numbers, too. In a battle, more cannonballs are better than fewer cannonballs, and it helps to know how many you have to work with. Plus, the last thing you want aboard your warship, battle or no battle, is loose cannonballs rolling around the deck.

It probably didn't matter to Sir Walter Raleigh if the cannonball pile looked pretty, but we know that tidy piles would have made Sara very happy.

When the Apollo Lunar Module landed on the Moon in 1969, the engineers intended for the landing struts – the "legs" of the Lunar Module – to be partially crushed, in a controlled manner. They wanted the struts to absorb the impact of the landing so that the lunar module itself didn't become damaged. The lower half of the Lunar Module – the Descent Stage – was left behind on the Moon, so the landing struts were only used once. As well as being deformable in a predicable way, the landing struts also had to be very light. That's because blasting material into space is expensive, and it becomes progressively more expensive as the weight is increased.

In designing the struts, the engineers had to optimize them for the task of absorbing impact. What do you think the objective function and the constraints might have been?

The optimization problem could have been set up to try to make the structure the lightest weight possible that could absorb the impact of the module landing on the Moon.

When we write "lightest weight possible" that means that the objective function is the weight, and we are trying to minimize it, or make it as small as possible.

When we write "that can absorb the impact of the module landing" that means a constraint is that the struts had to be able to prevent the module itself from getting damaged during the landing – no slamming into the Moon's surface.

The optimum solution the engineers found was a honeycomb structure.

The landing struts are made up of many long vertical cylinders with a hexagonal cross-section, and the cylinders were arranged in a hexagonal grid – another example of a space-filling tessellation. This structure is very lightweight, because each of the hexagonal cross-section cylinders is hollow.

The picture below shows, on the righthand side, a cross-section of one of the landing struts.

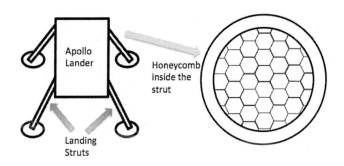

The landing module lands vertically on its struts, so during the landing the hexagonal cylinders in the struts are being pushed from both ends, along their length. It takes a lot of energy to crush the strut in that direction.

To get a feeling for this, take the cardboard tubes from two empty toilet paper rolls.

Put one of them down flat as shown on the left below. Put your hand on it and push down across its width, as the green arrow shows.

You'll feel that the tube crushes rather easily.

Then stand the other tube up and put your palm over its top. Push straight down along its length, as shown by the red arrow. You'll find that when the tube is positioned this way, it requires a lot more force before it buckles.

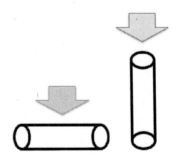

These tubes have circular cross sections, rather than hexagonal, but you can see that it takes more force to crush a tube along its length than across its width. That is why the Apollo lander was intended to land on its honeycomb clusters of hexagonal tubes that could absorb the impact along their length. But the engineers who built the lander also thought about pressure from the sides. They designed the struts so that even if they were being squashed from the side, their hexagonal cross-section tubes arranged in a hexagonal grid would be much stronger than a simple circular tube.

In these different problems (stacking cannonballs and creating crushable struts for the lunar module), the optimization problems have some very different objective functions (maximizing the number of balls and minimizing the weight, or maximizing the energy absorbed during crushing) and very different constraints (stability, prettiness, cost, weight).

TESSELLATION IN NATURE:

What do flowers, pineapple rinds, tortoise shells, the retina in the eye, soap bubbles and beehives all have in common?

By now you know the answer – tessellations!

Tessellations pop up in nature in many places. Some of them are more or less two dimensional (retina, tortoise shells) and others are three dimensional (soap bubbles). Some are very regular (beehives) and others are not at all regular (soap bubbles again).

One of the most obvious is with bees and their honeycombs. Bees produce a kind of wax which they make into hexagonal cells, with all sides the same length. The hexagonal cells in the honeycomb are used to store honey, pollen and larvae.

The cells are amazingly uniform regular hexagons – row after row after row all the same size and shape.

Why do bees make regular hexagonal grids?

Well, first of all, it makes sense that bees would want to have no gaps between cells, because gaps would be wasted space. Also, it would be a good idea to have a regular tessellation, where there is some repeating shape. If each bee could make whatever odd shape she wanted, then the other bees might have to wait for the first bee to finish her work, to see what weird thing she came up with, before knowing how to construct the next cell to attach to that previous one.

By using a repeating shape, lots of bees can work on building the hive at the same time, all of them knowing the shape they need to work on.

So far this makes sense, to say that the shape should have no gaps and it should be repeated over and over. But still, why hexagons? It could be triangles, or squares, or even something unusual like the lightning bolt from the earlier page, so long as all the bees did the same thing.

Scientists today do *not* think the reason that beehives are hexagons is because bees have six legs. That is what the ancient Roman author Pliny the Elder wrote more than 2000 years ago in his encyclopedia *Naturalis Historia.*

Mistake! Sometimes nature just has coincidences.

The answer is that the hexagon minimizes the amount of wax used in the walls. The bees did not actually sit down and write an optimization problem: *Design a regular tessellation that minimizes the amount of wax used to construct the walls, given a constraint on the cell size.* But somehow, presumably through evolution and natural selection, bees came up with the hexagonal cells that form a honeycomb, which does in fact minimize the perimeter per cell. Some other animals have figured this out too.

For example, a fish called tilapia also constructs for its eggs nice little hexagons that look just like honeycomb. Maybe we should call that fishcomb!

208

TESSELLATIONS AND ERROR CORRECTION CODING:

In the first book in this series –*The Secret Code Menace* – Sara, Daniel, and Jared learned about error correction coding. Error correction coding is related to tessellations.

We can think of this as packing balls into a space. With error correction coding, the balls are mathematical constructions in space, not actually physical balls.

Consider the very simple triplicate encoder. When you want to send a 0, you send three zeroes: 000. And when you want to send a 1, you send three ones: 111.

Suppose you have sent 000 and one of the bits is wrong. The recipient receives 001. The recipient can take a majority vote among the three bits received and decide that 0 wins. So, they will correctly work out that you sent a 0.

We can picture this operation in three-dimensional space.

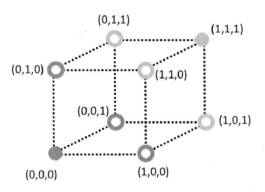

Here, the filled-in blue circle represents the codeword 000, with coordinates (0,0,0) in three-dimensional space.

The three blue circles that are not filled have distance 1 from the (0,0,0) point and represent the three possible states having a single bit in error, starting from the (0,0,0) codeword.

In the opposite corner the filled-in orange circle represents the codeword 111 with coordinates (1,1,1) in three-dimensional space.

The three open orange circles have distance 1 from the (1,1,1) point and they represent the three possible states having 1 bit in error starting from that codeword.

The majority vote is performed simply by taking a step from an open circle (a codeword received in error) to the closest of the filled-in circles (the valid codewords).

Here we have only two valid codewords, 000 and 111, so there is not a whole lot of "packing" going on.

But we can still think of each valid codeword as being as the center of a region of space that belongs to it.

If the received word comes out anywhere in the region of space that belongs to 000, then it gets decoded to 0.

If the received word comes out in the region of space that belongs to 111, then it gets decoded to 1.

Real error correction coding involves mathematical spaces that have more than three dimensions, so we can't make a picture of them. Since we can only picture three dimensions, we can't really make a mental picture of sphere packing in, say, eight-dimensional space.

But that is what happens with an error correction code. We can think of the codeword that is sent, for example, 1101101, as being a point at the center of a sphere.

That sphere is in a high-dimensional space.

When an error occurs in that codeword, the received codeword is another point in the high-dimensional space.

If that point is still within that same sphere, then the error correction code can correct the error and move back to the center of that sphere.

But if the error is very large (too many digits get changed) the point jumps over the boundary and may be inside a different sphere.

In this case, the error correction code will not resolve it to the right codeword.

How well the spheres pack together in the high-dimensional space is an important consideration in determining how much information can be sent with that code.

So some communication engineers spend a lot of time working on sphere packing!

PACKING FRACTION:

In two dimensions, when we put coins flat down on a table with no overlaps, the packing fraction is defined to be the area covered by coins divided by the total area. So, it is the fraction of the area which is covered by coins.

The packing fraction is always a number between zero and one. It equals zero when there are no coins on the table. And it equals one when the entire area is completely covered by a perfect layer of coins with no gaps in between.

This could happen if we had square coins that arranged together perfectly in a square tessellation.

QUESTION:

Suppose you have a square table on which you put one very large coin (circle) as shown below on the left, or you can fill the table with four coins (circles) as shown below on the right.

Which one has a larger packing fraction?
Or are the packing fractions the same?

(The answer is at the very end.)

The same kind of definition of packing fraction applies in three dimensions. When we drop a bunch of balls into a box, the packing fraction is defined as the volume of space occupied by the balls, divided by the total volume in the box. So, it is the fraction of the total space occupied by the balls.

We could use the same kind of definition for a suitcase. But there we usually have soft things like clothing which squish together and fill up the whole space, so the packing fraction is usually equal to 1.

If you stuff way too many things into your suitcase, you may break it. In that case, you can try telling your parents that you just wanted to know if it was possible to get a packing fraction larger than 1.

(Answer: it's not. That's why the suitcase broke.)

RANDOM PACKING FRACTION:

The random packing fraction is the fraction of the space that is occupied when you just drop stuff in the box randomly instead of carefully arranging it in a regular tessellation.

When coins are dropped randomly on a table, or balls are dropped randomly in the box, we don't know exactly how they will land.

In this case, as we saw in the M&M example in the story, we don't know exactly how the gaps will come out.

In ancient times, a buyer of barley might say to a merchant, "I want to buy one sack of grain." The merchant pours the grain into the sack. Pouring the grain in is random packing.

If the barley was sold as "one full sack", the seller would want the random packing to be as loose as possible, so the sack could look "full" but would have as little barley as possible in it. The buyer, on the other hand, would want to give

216

the sack a shake, so that the contents would settle. It would still be random packing, but it would become a *denser* random packing, requiring more barley in the sack in order for the sack to look "full".

The buyer and the seller have opposite goals in how they would like the density of the random packing to come out.

Today, when you buy breakfast cereal, there is random packing inside the box. One could still think about the packing fraction.

So, is it still worth shaking the cereal box to get the contents to settle into a denser packing?

Do the buyer and seller have opposite goals on how they would like the density of the random packing to come out?

Not really, because a cereal box is usually sold based on *weight*. It doesn't matter whether there is a loose or dense random packing inside the box, because, either way, the price is set based on how much the cereal weighs, not on the packing fraction.

RADIO FREQUENCY IDENTIFICATION (RFID):

RFID tags are little tags that get attached to objects to keep track of them. Today, RFID tags are used for many, many things. Equipment in a hospital may have tags so that doctors know where to find a machine regardless of what room it gets moved to.

Runners in a marathon have RFID tags to keep track of when they reach the finish line (and also to track that they didn't sneak off the course and take a shortcut). Some cars use RFID tags to pay tolls. The driver doesn't have to stop at a toll booth because the RFID tag makes sure that the driver's account is charged for the toll automatically as the car passes through the toll booth or under the scanner on the highway.

Library books may have RFID tags. Instead of opening each book and scanning each bar code, RFID tags enable a whole stack of books to be identified at once, without opening any of them.

How do RFID tags work?

There are two basic types: active and passive.

An active RFID tag has a battery and a little radio. It puts out a little radio signal every once in a while, to announce "I'm here. And this is what I am." If there is any RFID reader machine nearby, the signal from the tag contacts the reader regularly, so people searching for the object can find it.

A passive RFID tag does not have a battery, so it does not have the power by itself to send out a signal. But the RFID *reader* can send out a strong signal, called an *interrogating* signal. When the passive RFID tag receives an interrogating signal from the reader, it takes a little bit of power from the signal itself and then reflects some of the signal back, modified to indicate "I'm here. And this is what I am."

In the story, the owners of Mistral are thinking of putting in an RFID system to track the perfume bottles. That is a realistic use for RFID tags. For expensive items like perfume, each bottle could have its own tag. That way, if the wrong number of bottles were put into a shipping box, the RFID reader would know that the count was wrong.

ANSWERS:

Names of shapes:

Triangle, square, pentagon, hexagon, and octagon.

Tree shapes:

When you design a tree shape that will tessellate the plane perfectly with no gaps, the disadvantage is that you might not get the specific pretty tree shape you want.

For example, you wouldn't be able to tessellate a tree shape with lots of separate branches spreading out.

Likewise, you wouldn't have much chance of tessellating a tree shape with lots of fruit hanging down.

So, by adding the constraint that the shape has to tessellate, you are strongly constraining what kind of tree shapes you can have.

Packing fractions:

They have the same packing fraction.

When you fit a circle inside a square, the packing fraction is the area of the circle divided by the area of the square.

For the picture on the left, there is one big circle inscribed within one big square.

For the case on the right, think of it as four small circles inscribed within four small squares.

But the packing fraction for each of those four separately is the same as for the big one, so the packing fraction for the group of four is also the same.